SKOL! VIKING BLONDE ALE

FORTUNES, LOVE & FATE

ROSE MARIE MEUWISSEN

INTRODUCTION

Get ready to meet Inga, Nora, Katie, Gwen, Violet and Stephanie in a six-book series of contemporary sweet romance!

Fortunes, Love & Fate!

Six exciting sweet novellas linked by a unifying theme. You'll want to read each one!

FORTUNES, LOVE & FATE SERIES

Was it fate or merely a coincidence?

Six members of the Romancing the Lakes Book Club meet monthly at the Main Street Bookstore. This week, however, there's a huge community celebration going on and they decide, instead, to stroll through the Street Market where they encounter a fortune teller. She foretells they'll each find love. Will their fortunes come true?

This is Inga's story...

Inga was living the dream, planning events for her own company, Unique Events, but she still hadn't found a guy who could be 'The One' for her. She never would've believed a fortune from a gypsy fortune teller promising her a 'love that surpasses time' could come true.

Erik moved from Norway to Minnesota to expand his Nordic Brewing company in the U.S. He'd promised himself to devote all his time to the business, but how was he to know that an unknown force of fate would introduce him to a woman he couldn't walk away from?

Their attraction could not be denied because ultimately, they were destined to be together. But could the Atlantic Ocean keep them apart? Would that even be possible if they were truly soul mates?

Find all Fortunes, Love & Fate novellas at Amazon!
Skol! Viking Pale Ale by Rose Marie Meuwissen
Scarecrow by Ingrid Anderson-Sampo
Love in the Moonlight by Kathleen Nordstrom
Flirting with Frankenstein by Peg Pierson
The Gypsy's Curse by Ann Nardone
Dark Fortune by Denise Devine

ROSE MARIE MEUWISSEN

SKOL! VIKING BLONDE ALE

Fortunes, Love & Fate Series

Skol! Viking Blonde Ale

Fortunes, Love & Fate Series

Print Edition
Copyright 2020 by Rose Marie Meuwissen

ISBN Print Edition 978-0-9903788-3-9

Published in the United States of America

Nordic Publishing LLC

Cover Design by Raine English

❀ Created with Vellum

INGA'S FORTUNE:

Someone from your past will reappear in your life.
Your true soul mate.
With him, you will experience a love that surpasses time.

PROLOGUE

JAMES J. HILL DAYS IN WAYZATA ON LAKE MINNETONKA

SEPTEMBER

Inga pulled into the back-parking lot of Main Street Books at six. She couldn't believe it wasn't later. Friday night rush hour traffic on the 494 Freeway was bumper to bumper all the way from Eden Prairie to Wayzata. The weather was still holding its summer like temps and true Minnesotans would never pass up a beautiful autumn weekend to go up North to their cabins one last time before winter arrived. Today was the James J. Hill Days celebration in Wayzata and the main street was packed with people as she made her way into the book store to find her *Romancing the Lakes of Minnesota* book club. This month instead of their regular meeting, they planned to enjoy walking around and checking out the celebration. Probably was a good call, she thought, since it would've been difficult to hold their meeting in the crowded book store and the activity outside would've been immensely distracting.

"Am I the last one to arrive?" Inga asked as she approached the book club group standing in front of the latest arrival shelf where the romance section was located.

"Bet the traffic was awful," Nora stated.

"Ready, to brave the crowds?" Katie asked.

"I'm hungry and thirsty, let's go!" Violet said.

Inga nodded in agreement and followed the group out the door to Main Street. They made their way down the street stopping at booths to look at the novelties for sale until finally, they stopped at the end of the street where the most unusual trailer was parked. The sign above the open door read, 'Fortune Teller'. It appeared to be Vintage, but these days they could make anything look old, even if it was new. Although, she had to admit, she'd never seen anything like it before, even though she'd been to many events. After all, she was an event planner. Intrigued was putting it mildly. Unfortunately, there was no stopping her curiosity. So, she entered the trailer.

"Come in, please," a very thickly accented voice beckoned from inside the trailer.

"Hello." Inga ducked and stepped into the trailer, taking in all the antiques and draped surroundings.

"Take a seat," the lady in gypsy like garb directed. "Let me see what your life has in store for you."

Inga didn't believe in fortune telling, at least she didn't think she did, but what could it possibly hurt to oblige the lady. It might be worth a laugh later, so she sat down on the partially pulled out chair at the table.

The fortune teller took the seat across from Inga and reached for her hand.

Slowly, Inga extended her hand. When their hands touched, Inga felt a strange sensation flow through her entire body, almost like a spark of electricity. It only lasted a few seconds and then was gone. She had no idea what it was or what caused it, but she finally relaxed.

The woman's face seemed deep in thought and completely fixated on her hand. "You are a very special lady. Very strong and independent. I see happiness in your future."

"Do you see a man?" Inga wasn't sure why'd she'd asked that particular question.

"Yes." The woman continued staring at her hand. "A very handsome man."

"Well, there certainly are enough good-looking men around. What I need is one that is interested in me long enough to stick around for a while."

"You have not met 'The One' yet."

"When? When will it happen? I'm getting really tired of waiting around for him."

"Soon."

"So, is that my fortune?"

"No." The woman hesitated, then picked up a piece of paper and wrote a few lines down on it. She handed it to Inga. "This is your fortune: *Someone from your past will reappear in your life. Your true soul mate. With him, you will experience a love that surpasses time.*"

"Great. But I'm sorry, I don't believe in magic."

"That's okay you don't have to believe. It will happen anyway."

Their eyes locked for a moment.

Inga got up to leave. "How much do I owe you?" Inga asked.

"For you, no charge. I've been waiting for you."

"I don't understand."

The fortune teller waived her hand in a shooing motion, indicating Inga was done and should leave.

As Inga stepped out of the trailer, Katie rushed up the steps. "My turn."

"So, what do you think? Is the Fortune Teller legit?" Violet asked.

"What kind of a question is that? Of course, it's not real. No one can tell another person what will happen in their future," Stephanie said.

"Care to share?" Nora asked.

Inga handed the piece of paper to Violet, who in turn handed it to Stephanie, who in turn handed it to Gwen and lastly to Nora.

"At least it's a good fortune. Let's hope it comes true," Stephanie said.

"Come on, you're not buying into this stuff, are you?" Inga shook her head.

Minutes later, Katie came down the trailer's steps, paper in hand grinning from ear to ear.

Violet practically ran to the steps to be next.

Each romance book club member shared their fortune while the next one took their turn. Being romantics at heart, they were all thrilled to find romance in their fortunes.

They continued strolling leisurely down the other side of the street where the craft brewery tents were located.

Inga spotted a tent with *Nordic Brewing* as the name. She selected it out of the five tents because of her love for all things Nordic and Viking. In fact, the Viking Ship logo caught her eye first. She walked up to the counter to see the menu more closely.

"What can I get you?"

Inga looked up quickly when she heard the strong Norwegian accented English and to her surprise saw almost a '*Thor*' look alike, only his blonde hair was shorter. He could very well be from Viking blood, she thought. *Tall, muscular, with a chiseled face. Have I just died and gone to Valhalla?*

"What can I get you?" he repeated smiling broadly at her.

"What would you suggest?" she managed to get out. "I've never tried your brand before."

"For you lovely lady, I'd suggest the Viking Blonde Ale."

"Sounds absolutely perfect."

He turned his broad toned back toward her stretching the black T-shirt taut against his muscles and filled a plastic souvenir cup with Valhalla printed on one side and a picture of a Viking on the other side.

Inga pulled a five-dollar bill from her purse and set it on the counter. He handed her the cup instead of setting it down and her fingers lightly brushed his in the process. *There it was again.* A shiver of sorts shimmied its way through her body.

"Thank you, hope you enjoy it," he said as he picked up the money to put in the cash register.

"Thanks, I'm sure I will," Inga said while her eyes lingered on this modern-day Viking man. She felt sad that she would most likely not ever see him again. *Oh well, one can only wish.* She turned and walked away spotting her friends up ahead at a different craft brewery tent.

CHAPTER 1

"I give up. I'm giving up dating." Inga Pederson set her phone down gently, even though what she wanted to do was throw it across the room. Luckily, the sensible part of her emphasized that the cost of a new phone was not in her current budget.

"Did he just cancel on you again?" her friend and business partner, Karoline Wagner, asked as she walked into Inga's office.

"Yes. It's the third time in two weeks."

"When is the last time you saw him?" Karoline asked as she sat down in the chair across from Inga.

"Two weeks ago. Do you think I tried to move too quickly?" Inga asked.

"Yes."

"Really?"

"Yes. I know how badly you wanted a date for the Halloween event, but I have to say, I just didn't get good vibes about Tom. He wasn't really your type."

"You're right. I just didn't want to be the only one alone at the event."

"I'm sure you won't be. It's not a couple's event, anyway. There should be lots of single people in attendance. Maybe, you'll meet someone there. I know you'll find a guy who is right for you, but it just isn't today. And it certainly wasn't Tom."

"Why are you so smart? And how do you know exactly the right things to say?" Inga asked.

"Hey, what are friends for? We support each other." Karoline smiled and gently touched Inga's hand.

Inga dabbed at the corner of her eye where a tear had threatened to fall, but hadn't. Karoline was absolutely right. Tom was a jerk. She'd known it from the first day she'd met him. And deep down, she knew she was trying too hard to find her soul mate. She needed to just let it happen naturally. "Sorry, for the drama. Haven't we got an event to plan?" Inga stood up and reached for a folder sitting on the cabinet next to her desk.

"I see you've been working on it already. Show me!" Karoline exclaimed.

"I know there's been a lot of hype about the Vikings recently and after all, we do have a team named the Vikings, so I thought maybe we could go with something new that hasn't been done before. The theme would be *Skol on All Hallow's Eve*."

"I like it! It's totally different. What did you have in mind?" Karoline asked.

"Since it's the apple orchard's event and they are sponsoring it, we should definitely have it there. We could use their parking lot and put up large tents. Get a few food trucks to come in but we would specify the foods we want served. Also, vendors with themed items for sale. And of course, a band for dancing. The orchard would need to get a temporary liquor license."

"Wow, you should get dumped more often, might just be when you do your best work! I love it! Let's get to work." Karoline smiled.

"I'll put together the proposal and get it sent off this morning."

"The event is in a little over four weeks, so we need to move quickly on this. I'm going to check out the food trucks available for that date. So, you have a food list in mind?"

"Right here. Viking stew-Lapskaus, Mini-Apple pies deep fried, and Onion hay stacks for starters. A witch's brew caldron, hence the liquor license. Or maybe, a small craft brewery with Viking Ale." Inga pulled out the food list she'd printed and handed it to Karoline.

"Olav's cousin has a new company he just recently started in the U.S. It makes various kinds of beer and ale. The one they want to try first in Minnesota is a Viking Ale Brew. It just may be exactly what we're looking for to complete the theme of our event."

"Sounds perfect. Can you talk to him?"

"On it. Say, you should meet him. He's available and good looking, at least I think so. But then again, he is Olav's cousin and I may be a bit biased since I think my Olav is one hot guy. They are from Norway which means they both come from Viking blood."

"Great, Karoline! I'm swearing off dating and men, then here you are, telling me I need to meet a guy from Norway who just happens to make Viking Ale."

"You're absolutely right. You should wait a little bit at least before you try dating again. He'll be arriving back in the states on Thursday, does that work for you?" Karoline started laughing and made a quick dash for the door before Inga reconsidered throwing something at her.

"Very funny, Karoline. But after some consideration, I think next week will be fine. It'll just be a business meeting. Not a date!" Inga called out as she stood at her door.

"I heard that. I'll have Olav set up a meeting sometime next week and I'll let you know the day and time. Hopefully, on Monday."

CHAPTER 2

Late Tuesday morning, Inga and Karoline arrived downtown at the weekly *Lunch with Food Trucks* event on the Nicollet Mall. After parking, they strolled down the Mall taking in all the food trucks and their menus.

"I don't think we're going to find one that has Lapskaus on the menu," Karoline stated.

"Probably not, but we need to find one who'd be willing to do a special menu for us." Inga kept walking and made a straight line to a food truck she spied on the end named, *Nordic Treats.*

Karoline eventually noticed Inga had left her standing in front of an Asian Food Truck and immediately followed her down the street. "Who would've believed we would find a Nordic food truck?" Karoline stared at the menu. "Lapskaus isn't on the menu, but that doesn't mean they couldn't make it."

A cute young blonde woman came over to the counter. "Can I help you?"

"I certainly hope so. My name is Inga and this is Karoline. We are event planners and are planning an outdoor Halloween event at an apple orchard in town. The theme is *Skol on All Hallow's Eve.*"

A smile spread across the woman's face. "Sounds intriguing. What kind of food are you serving?"

"We'd like to serve Lapskaus, a type of Viking stew. Are you familiar with it?" Inga asked.

"Oh, yes! I love it and we have served it before. I grew up eating it. Oh, by the way, my name is Tovi Sunstol."

"Would you be available on Saturday, October 30?" Karoline asked.

"Yes, that happens to be at the end of our season and the weather is kind of iffy around Halloween, so I didn't take any jobs that week. It can be a gorgeous 70 degrees or a snowstorm. Do you have plans in case it's bad weather?"

"We did take that into consideration when planning the event. The apple orchard has two large pole barns. They wouldn't fit the food trucks but the people would be inside. We can have the food trucks parked by the entrance doors though, so they wouldn't have to go far for food," Inga eagerly replied. "Sounds like you are well prepared." Tovi reached under the counter, grabbed her marketing literature and handed it to Inga. "All my info is in here. Just send me an email with the details if you are interested in having Nordic Treats at the event."

"Oh, we want you. Finding your food truck is a miracle. It's just what we were looking for," Karoline responded.

"Well, thank you. There are only a couple of Scandinavian food trucks in the Twin Cities which is unusual since there are really a lot of Scandinavians in Minnesota. I'm glad you found mine."

"Great," Karoline said and handed her their business card. "I will be sending you a contract to look over. Our company name is Unique Events."

"Say if you will be serving any alcohol," Tovi said. "I recently heard of a new craft brewery in town called Nordic Brewing. They have a new offering called Viking Blonde Ale that would fit perfectly with your theme."

"Funny you should mention them. I saw them at the James J. Hill Days event in Wayzata. And yes, we will be serving alcohol and they are on our list of craft breweries to contact," Inga replied as a huge smile spread across her face, remembering the Thor look alike who had served her a beer.

"I'm not serving Lapskaus today." Tovi stated. "But let me give you a sample of our Norwegian Almond Cake dessert."

Inga and Karoline watched Tovi prepare two small plates each with a slice of almond cake, a spoonful of whipped cream topped with lingonberries.

"Enjoy," Tovi said and handed them each a plate.

"Thanks, we'll be in contact," Inga said and they walked away to allow the customers who were lined up behind them to get to the counter and place their orders.

"Thanks," Karoline said.

They walked over to a table and sat down to enjoy their dessert.

"This is delicious," Inga said as she devoured the Nordic delicacy.

"Have you ever had this before?" Karoline savored the almond flavor.

"Yes. My grandmother used to make it. Isn't it great?" Inga asked.

"I should get this recipe and try making it for my Norwegian boyfriend," Karoline commented.

"Sounds good. Be sure to invite me over for a sample to see if you did it right," Inga laughed.

"You should learn how to make it, too. Heck, you're the one who is Norwegian. Do you have a recipe from your grandmother?" Karoline asked.

"I'll ask my mother if she has it," Inga said.

"Who knows, you might be getting a Norwegian boyfriend soon, too."

"Whatever! I just swore off men, remember?"

They finished their cake and meandered down the rest of the street looking for a food truck to make hay stacks.

"What exactly are you envisioning for the hay stacks?" Karoline asked.

"Not sure exactly. Maybe those skinny onion rings in a pile that would resemble a stack of hay?" Inga motioned with her hands in a jester of what a pile would look like.

"Got it." Karoline nodded. "Or maybe some type of hash brown potatoes? They would make a nice pile."

They both laughed. Up ahead was a *Tator Tot* food truck.

"What do you think?" Inga pointed at the truck.

"I'm assuming you're thinking they might be able to make potato stacks. I thought you wanted onions?" Karoline continued walking. "Let's keep looking. Hey, that one does onion rings. *The Onion Blossom,* nice name."

"I think the skinny onion rings are called onion strings and they would look more like hay stacks. Okay, let's ask them if they can make onion strings," Inga said.

"Can I help you ladies?" an older man behind the counter greeted them.

"I'm Karoline and this is Inga. We're looking to hire a food truck for a special event, but we need a specific food served."

"And what would that be?" he asked.

"I believe they are called onion strings. I see you do onion rings. Would you be able to make onion strings?" Inga asked.

The man looked a bit bewildered at their request.

"We're event planners and are planning a Halloween event on October 30. We want the onion strings because we want them to look like hay stacks," Karoline offered.

"Oh, I see." He looked at his wife who was back by one of the deep fryers. "What do you think?"

She nodded in approval.

"I guess that's a yes." He reached under the counter and handed Inga their menu with a business card. "I'm John Schafer. You can send me all the info by email."

"Thanks, our company name is Unique Events, we'll be in touch." Karoline handed him a card.

They walked down the street past the rest of the food trucks.

"I'm hungry," Inga said as she looked at all the choices surrounding them. "Let's get something to eat."

"We had dessert first, so let's get the main course now." Karoline continued walking down the row of food trucks.

"I saw taco salads when we first started our search," Inga suggested.

"Sounds good to me." Karoline nodded. "I think we made good progress today. We found two food trucks that will serve exactly what you wanted. Did you already talk to the apple orchard about the apple pies?"

"Yes, in fact, they said fried apple pies were something they'd been thinking about trying to sell so this would be the perfect opportunity to test them out," Inga replied.

"Great, now we just need the alcohol."

"That meeting is next Monday, right?" Inga asked.

"Yes, I talked to Olav and he has us all set up for 10 a.m. on Monday morning." Karoline stopped in front of the Taco food truck.

CHAPTER 3

Inga arrived at the apple orchard on Wednesday in the pouring rain to check out the pole barn buildings. They were nice enough and they would definitely be using them. Heck, if it wasn't raining or snowing, it could still be quite cool outside. It could also be sunny and seventy, which would be much preferable. Oh well, whatever they got, she would make sure the event was perfect.

"Inga, so glad to see you. How are all the plans going for my Viking themed event?" Darla, the owner of Jensrud Apple Orchard, greeted Inga.

"Great! I'm excited for this event. So far, we have booked the two food trucks we agreed on. We have *Nordic Treats* that will be serving the Lapskaus and *The Onion Blossom* that will be serving onion strings aka onion hay stacks."

"Wow, I'm impressed you found someone who could make the Lapskaus. We experimented with the mini fried apple pies and they are delicious. I had the kitchen make some fresh ones today so you can try one."

Thankfully, the rain stopped and the sun now peeked through the clouds. Inga and Darla made their way around the puddles to the main building where the store and kitchen were located.

At the bakery counter, the clerk handed Inga a mini fried apple pie to sample.

It was still warm when she took a bite and was like biting into a piece of apple heaven. "I love it! Good job, guys!"

"My sentiments exactly. We are adding them to the bakery menu next week. They will be available with different toppings. Whipped Cream sprinkled with Cinnamon, Carmel topping, Crushed Walnuts and for the Nordic theme –almond flavored ice cream sprinkled with Cardamom."

"Wow, those all sound delicious. I may have to try them all. But this one tastes great plain, too."

"You'll definitely have to try the Nordic topping version. The three flavors blend together for an exquisite taste," Darla explained.

"Oh, you count on me to try it," Inga said while taking the last bite. "Any luck with a band you liked?"

Darla nodded. "My cousin gave me the name of a group called Scandik Blues. He said they have a few Blues songs that are sort of eerie and would be perfect for Halloween. Some are considered Viking chants from back in the Viking era. Plus, a bunch of regular blues and even some Rock-n-Roll songs. I visited their website to listen to some of the songs and they sounded good. I'll send you a link so you can check out their music."

"Great. I'll listen to their music, but what matters most is that you like it, after all it is your apple orchard's event," Inga said.

"Okay. We're just waiting to get everything finalized before we order the advertising."

"Yes, the clock is ticking. We're meeting with a craft brewery on Monday. You'll love this, Darla. Their name is Nordic Brewing and they have a new offering called Viking Blonde Ale."

"This is all coming together beautifully. I'm so glad I found someone who also loves all this Viking stuff like I do." Darla could barely contain the excitement in her voice for the upcoming Fall Harvest event at her apple orchard.

"Hopefully, we will be able to have firm contracts in hand by Tuesday next week and then you can have your advertising people insert the names of the food vendors, craft brewer and the band," Inga stated.

"Thanks for all your hard work on this event. Now we just have to keep our fingers crossed for good weather."

~

On the way home, Inga couldn't stop thinking about the fortune given by the gypsy fortune teller.

Someone from your past will reappear in your life.

Your true soul mate.

With him, you will experience a love that surpasses time.

She'd read it over and over till she'd memorized it. And it was totally unintentional. Why this fortune intrigued her so much was a mystery. She didn't even believe in fortune telling. Heck, it was simply a commercial hoax to give people hope that something good would happen in their love life and a way to make money in the process. What she couldn't understand was the reason for the gypsy refusing her money. It was odd, since charging money for telling fortunes was the way they made their living. She couldn't help remembering the strange sensation that had flowed through her entire body when the gypsy touched her hand. It was a sensation she'd never experienced before. Did it mean something? Maybe there was something wrong with her? Maybe she was sick?

The whole thing was weird. As for the fortune, who could possibly reappear from her past? She'd never even had a steady boyfriend. And what the heck was a love that could surpass time? Did that mean Time Travel? Everyone knew that wasn't real. Well, at least she didn't think it was.

Thinking about the fortune coming true was just plain stupid. She hadn't even told Karoline because it was definitely not likely to actually happen.

Now on the other hand, the guy working in the Nordic Brewing tent was real and he was so darn good looking. He was something that could happen! And she would definitely like it if it did!

CHAPTER 4

It was one of those TGIF days. Not that it had been a bad week, but she'd worked her tail off getting all the arrangements set and contracts signed for the apple orchard's Halloween event. The food was a major item on the list, but there had been a long list of other things, too. They needed tents, tables, chairs, decorations, heaters, fire pits, lighting, signage and the list went on. All that was left was the band and the craft brewery.

Scandik Blues had a very nice website, which she'd checked out thoroughly. Tonight, they were playing at *Valhalla Nordic Smoke and Ale House* located near White Bear Lake. The bar was sponsoring a Viking costume event with large dollar cash prizes-$250-for the best male and female costumes. The band had CD's available on the website with thirty second samples to listen to. One of the songs on their Viking Blues CD was called *Helvegen* which was described as a Viking funeral song. It was hauntingly beautiful and would be perfect for her event, so she downloaded the song to her phone so Karoline could listen to it.

Inga walked down the hall to Karoline's office. "Got a minute?"

"Sure, have a seat."

"I want you to listen to this song by Scandik Blues." Inga tapped her phone to play the song and sat down while they listened.

"I love it! It will be perfect. Are they available?" Karoline asked.

"Strangely, their calendar doesn't show they are booked that day. I sent a request to have someone contact me, so I'll let you know."

"Your Nordic theme seems to be working out well, Inga."

"Do you have any plans for the evening? They are playing tonight in White Bear Lake."

"Sorry, I have a hair appointment tonight."

"Not a problem, I'll see if Jackie wants to go check out a band with me." Inga's phone rang. "It's the band getting back to me already."

"Hello," Inga answered and walked out of Karoline's office then down the hall to her office.

"This is Jon with Skandik Blues. Got your message. So, you're interested in possibly booking the band? What date are you looking for?"

"Saturday, October 30."

"The band is available that day."

"Great! I didn't think that date would be open, but I'm glad it is."

"The band was booked for that weekend, Friday and Saturday. At least that's what we thought, but due to a misunderstanding we just recently found out, they only needed a band on Friday. So, if you only need Saturday, you're in luck, Inga."

"The band is playing tonight at *Valhalla Nordic Smoke and Ale House* in White Bear Lake. I'm going to stop by tonight to listen to the music before I make a commitment to hire the band, if that's okay?"

"Wise decision. If you're into Viking things, you'll love it. The bar is hosting a Viking costume contest, so feel free to come dressed in Viking apparel. I'll be there so just ask for Jon and they will find me."

"I'll be the one dressed in jeans. Though, it sounds like it will be a great place to get Viking costume ideas, as I am looking to purchase one for our event. See you tonight."

Going to bars alone was not on her list of fun things to do. She quickly sent Jackie a text to see if she was free tonight. Only minutes later, Jackie texted back that she would meet her there at seven thirty. That was a relief! Now she was looking forward to the evening and checking out all the Viking costumes. From what she heard as far as the music was concerned, she really liked the samples on their website, so she was pretty sure a contract with the band would be signed tonight.

It was almost five and all her work was finished for the week. Where did one get a Viking costume? She wanted something that looked authentic, not a cheaply made Halloween type of costume.

The internet, that's where.

She googled Viking costumes to see what came up. Of course, the cheesy ones came up first, she kept scrolling and ended up on Etsy where there were some hand-made costumes more in line with what she was looking for. Listed was a variety of colors and sizes to choose from, along with full-length cloaks. This was probably the way to go, but first she wanted to check out the, hopefully, wide array of costumes entering the contest tonight.

Inga left the office and headed home to change into her skin tight but comfy jeans and a black V-neck t-shirt she'd ordered off the internet that said *I come from Viking Blood*. She'd found it on a website a year ago but had never worn it. Tonight seemed like an appropriate time to show it off. The people attending this event would appreciate it. Luckily, she'd learned how to braid her own hair, so she braided each side separately and then joined them in the back. Adding some dangly silver earrings completed the look, along with her black leather boots.

At nearly seven thirty, she parked her car down the street from the bar. Wow, it must be crowded, she thought. Cars were lined up and down the nearby streets and the parking lot was full. She made her way to the entrance to meet Jackie, who was already standing near the door waiting for her.

"You look great, Inga! Love the T-shirt!" Jackie said.

"Thanks. Got it a while ago, but this is the first time I've worn it. Felt like the appropriate time."

"My closet doesn't include Viking attire, so this will have to do." Jackie pointed to her jeans, Harley t-shirt and boots. Her petite trim body and long brown hair, lightly curled, exuded confidence and definitely said sexy.

"Maybe, Harley riders are the modern-day version of Vikings."

They couldn't help laughing as they walked inside the bar.

Inga walked up to the hostess counter where they were charging an entrance fee for the event. "Hi, my name is Inga and I'm looking for Jon with the band."

"Welcome, your name is on the list, so no entrance fee. You'll find him up in the sound booth."

"Thanks." Inga and Jackie walked into the bar area in search of Jon.

In the sound booth, they found a man with a chiseled face framed by a close-trimmed beard and short wavy black hair, setting up equipment.

"Hi, are you Jon?" Inga asked.

"Yes."

"I'm Inga and this is my friend, Jackie."

He stood up and shook her hand. "Good to meet you. I reserved a table in the restaurant for you in case you want to have dinner first. The food here is excellent, especially if you like meat. But the Fish and Chips are quite tasty, too. The band starts at nine and you're welcome to join me here in the sound booth then. There's a nice view from here and not nearly as crowded as it will be down on the dance floor once they begin playing."

"Thank you," Inga replied. "We were planning on having dinner first, so we'll take you up on the reserved table. And we'd love to join you here for the show."

"Great. Try to get over here by eight forty-five. Oh, and I wanted to ask if you have any song requests?" Jon asked.

"I'd like to hear *Helvegen*, if it wouldn't be any trouble."

"Oh, they'll be playing that song, it's always a favorite of the crowd, especially at any Viking events. You know the words are in Norwegian?"

"Yes. I am curious as to what the words translate to in English, though."

Jon reached into a file folder inside his bag, pulled out a sheet of

21

paper and handed it to her. "People always ask, so I had a bunch of these printed off to hand out. It's much easier than me trying to translate parts of the song for them. Takes much less time, too."

Inga graciously took the sheet. "Thanks, saves me the trouble of trying to find an English version online." She nodded and they left to find their reserved table in the restaurant section.

CHAPTER 5

"Wow, this is really cool," Jackie said. "It's like walking into a real Viking Hall. Love the Viking Shields and the way they're all different."

"Look at the war axes in this glass case. They look like the ones used in the Viking series on the History Channel. The long handles look as if to be made out of wood and the steel ax heads appear to be really sharp. I don't know how anyone survived being attacked by one of these." Inga continued staring into the case.

"Not many did. Sorry to intrude in your conversation. I'm Erik."

Inga recognized the voice behind her. But from where she wasn't sure. As soon as she turned to see who was speaking to her, she saw the chiseled face of Thor. Well, not Thor himself, but heck he could definitely pass for his double. It was the hunky man from the Nordic Brewing tent she'd met at the James J. Hill Days event.

Inga caught Jackie's nod to let her know she was going to check out the rest of the deco, allowing her some time alone with Erik.

She realized she was staring blatantly at him. Probably her mouth was hanging open, too. Something about this man was unusual, although strange as it was, she felt drawn to him for some odd reason. Oh, he was definitely hot and she wanted him more than she'd ever wanted any other guy she'd met. Oddly though, she didn't even know him.

Finally, she was able to speak, "I'm Inga." She extended her hand to shake his. When he did the same and their hands touched, she felt a rush travel through her body. Again. Maybe she actually did need to make a doctor's appointment. This just wasn't normal.

"I think we've met briefly before. You ordered a Viking Blonde Ale at the Nordic Brewing Tent in Wayzata during the James J. Hill Days event."

How could she forget? It was ingrained in her mind. "Yes, I remember. So, here we both are at another event. A Viking costume event with a Scandinavian band."

"I see you didn't want to be in the costume contest for the best Viking costume."

"I don't have a Viking costume. Yet. I want to get one but wasn't sure what style I liked, so I thought this would be a great place to check out local Viking costumes or attire."

"There certainly will be a variety of costumes here. I think you came to the right place."

"What you're wearing looks quite authentic." Inga gave his costume the once-over look.

"I had it made in Norway."

"Oh, so it is the real thing, then. I particularly like the cloak. And the Celtic looking pin appears to be vintage."

"Yes, it is. I found it on my family farm in Norway. It may very well be from the Viking Era."

"So, you live in Norway?"

"Yes, but I'm branching out my business and opening a location in the Minneapolis area."

She wasn't sure how that worked as far as being a citizen of one country and living even temporarily in another country. "One of my great-grandparent's came from Norway, but I've never been there. I've heard it's beautiful. One day, I'd like to visit the Land of the Vikings. I feel very drawn to anything Viking, which is why I'm here tonight."

"Are you staying to listen to the band play?"

"Yes, I'm very interested in hearing their music."

Jackie approached them. "Our table is ready."

"I will let you ladies have dinner. The cod is fresh and seasoned perfectly. I highly recommend it."

"It was nice to meet you, Erik."

"Is it okay if I catch up with you later for a dance?"

"Yes. See you a little later, then."

Erik bowed and walked away.

Inga and Jackie watched his tall six foot plus frame and muscular arms pull the cloak in place as he made his way toward the outside bar.

"Wow! What just happened? Do you know him? He's so hot!" Jackie rambled out question after question.

"Not really sure. I saw him at the James J. Hill Days event. He was working at a craft brewing tent called Nordic Brewing. He poured me a glass of Viking Blonde Ale. It was excellent. But anyway, when our hands touched as he handed me the beer or I guess its appropriate name is ale, I felt a strange tingling rush go through me. Not sure if he felt it too, or if I'm coming down with something, but I just experienced that same feeling again when he shook my hand a little bit ago."

"So, are you attracted to this man who is a dead ringer for Thor?"

"You'd have to be made of stone not to be."

"Did you give him your number?" Excitement radiated from Jackie's face.

"He didn't ask for it. Dang!"

"Well, he said he wanted to find you for a dance after the band starts playing, so we'll have to make sure he finds you and doesn't leave without your business card."

They sat down in a cozy booth adorned with Celtic scrolling on the bench backs and carved with Viking dragon heads. The table top showcased a Norwegian fjord scene of majestic white capped mountains overlooking the dark blue ocean water completely encased in a lacquer finish. They both picked up the menus already placed on the table.

"This is so great!" Inga didn't even try to curb her excitement. "All these dishes are Nordic themed. I love fish so I'm going to try the baked cod with potato slices. Erik recommended it."

"Oh, so Erik recommended it...Sounds like you like him."

"Maybe. Still deciding. I'll let you know."

"I'm going to try the Nordic Meatballs on a pile of mashed potatoes topped off with lingonberries. Sounds delicious!" Jackie set down her menu.

After the waiter, dressed in leather leggings and a billowy long shirt with a wide leather type belt took their orders, they checked out the English translation of Helvegen.

Wardruna – Helvegen Lyrics

Norwegian - English translation

Hvem skal synge meg - Who shall sing me

i daudsvevna slynge meg - into the death-sleep sling me

når eg på Helvegen går - When I walk on the Path of Death

og dei spora eg trår er kalda, så kalda - and the tracks I tread are cold, so cold

Eg songane søkte - I sought the songs

Eg songane sende - I sent the songs

då den djupaste brunni - when the deepest well

gav meg dråper så ramme - gave me the drops so touched

av Valfaders pant - of Death-fathers wager

Alt veit eg, Odin - I know it all, Odin

var du gjømde ditt auge - where you hid your eye

Hvem skal synge meg - Who shall sing me

i daudsvevna slynge meg - into the death-sleep sling me

når eg på Helvegen går - When I walk on the Path of Death

og dei spora eg trår er kalda, så kalda - and the tracks I tread are cold, so cold

Årle ell i dagars hell - early in the days end

enn veit ravnen om eg fell - still the raven knows if I fall

Når du ved Helgrindi star - When you stand by the Gate of Death

og når du laus deg må riva - And you have to tear free

skal eg fylgje deg - I shall follow you

over Gjallarbrua med min song - across the Resounding Bridge with my song

Du blir løyst frå banda som bind deg! - You will be free from the bonds that bind you!

Du er løyst frå banda som batt deg! - You are free from the bonds that bound you!

"That's pretty eerie! I see why it's a funeral song. Almost more unnerving when you don't know what it means. Have you ever heard it?" Inga asked.

"No, but I'm looking forward to hearing the song after reading this."

"It'll be interesting to see if they can do it justice since the Wardruna version is known for being so hauntingly beautiful."

"Doesn't sound like it would be dance music. Hopefully they play some other stuff that is. Wouldn't want you to miss out on your dance with *Thor.*"

The waiter appeared with their drinks. Two glasses engraved with Valhalla on the front side and filled with Viking Blonde Ale.

"This is the brand made by the Nordic Brewing company where Erik works, right?"

Inga took a drink, savoring the ale as it washed down her throat. "Yes, and I have to say it is darn good."

Jackie also took a drink. "I like it. Hopefully, they do well with it and sell a lot."

Their meals arrived quickly and they savored the flavors of the deliciously Nordic meals.

CHAPTER 6

E rik couldn't stop thinking about Inga. Her beautiful face
with the high cheekbones and sparkling blue eyes spoke
volumes of her Nordic heritage. The long blonde hair
framing flawless skin could very well match any young woman of her
age portrayed in a Viking Era painting. Speaking of age, he didn't
know how old she was but he would guess about thirty. From what he
could see, she obviously kept her trim body in shape. And, he'd definitely noticed her skin tight jeans. Conversation with her had been
easy. He'd been leery of getting involved with anyone in the U.S. since
he most likely would be going back to Norway. Although, he hadn't
missed her comment on wanting to visit Norway.

When they'd first met at the James J. Hill Days event at his Nordic
Brewery tent, he'd been in awe of her regal looking beauty. A lot of
women who possessed such attractiveness were so stuck up that a guy
couldn't even strike up a conversation with them. But not her, she'd
been very approachable, actually had asked for his suggestion on
which beer to choose. She'd even been so agreeable that she took his
suggestion and ordered the Viking Blonde Ale.

What he couldn't understand was the rush that flowed through his
body when their hands touched while he handed her the ale. He'd

never felt anything like it before. Being in his mid-thirties, he'd dated his fair share of women in Norway. Even the ones he'd felt infatuated with in his youth hadn't produced a rush similar to it.

And then tonight when he saw her standing in the bar area, he knew it was her even before she'd turned his way so he could see her face. He had no idea how, but he'd been sure it was her. Possibly a gut feeling? Striking up a conversation with an almost stranger was a bold move on his part but he couldn't resist the urge to talk to her. The reception on her part was definitely a God-send.

The handshake was unexpected and the resulting rush he'd felt again was exhilarating. In a way, it felt so familiar and deep inside his body a burning need to feel it again arose. He'd never felt the desire to commit to a woman before, but with Inga he felt comfortable and at home with to the point of wanting to claim her as his woman. Had he just thought that? What was wrong with him? This was the twentieth century and men did not claim women.

"Erik, sorry I'm late. It took me awhile to put together a Viking costume." Mark apologized and shook his hand.

"Looks good, I think." Erik gave him the once over look.

"Well, let's just say I gave up and decided to go with the Vikings Football theme instead." Mark displayed his attire complete with a purple Vikings jersey and a helmet with horns.

Erik laughed. "I guess in Minnesota that works."

"I see the Nordic Brewing banners promoting Viking Blonde Ale are all in place. They look good," Mark commented.

They walked up to the bar to get two cans of Viking Blonde Ale. Outside events required cans instead of bottles be sold to prevent broken bottles being disposed of improperly. It also eliminated the chance of someone falling and getting accidentally cut from the glass.

"Don't want to be dragging this around all night. I'm going to take my Viking cloak out to the car. Can you keep an eye on my ale until I get back?" Erik asked.

"Sure. I'll just be standing here checking out all the cool Viking costumes, getting ideas for next time." Mark grinned.

Erik couldn't help laughing. Mark, his business manager from the brewery, was in obvious search of a girlfriend. "It looks more like you are checking out the Valkyrie costumes."

On his way out, Erik needed to walk through the bar and past the entrance to the restaurant which was where Inga was enjoying her dinner. He couldn't resist a glance toward the table where she sat. Her smile was contagious as she talked and laughed with her friend. Dang, what was wrong with him? He was acting like a smitten teenage boy. He needed to get a grip on his obvious attraction to her. Unfortunately, there wasn't a remote possibility that he would be giving up his promised dance with her. Nothing was going to prevent that from happening. Not a chance in the world.

An hour later, the band took the stage, as he watched Inga and her friend take seats in the sound booth. This would make his approach for a dance more awkward than anticipated. Luckily, when the music filled the air, she left the sound booth to stand with the crowd. He couldn't take his eyes off her body as she moved slowly to the beat of the music. He felt immensely drawn to her, but he knew he had to use control. After all, it was only the first song and there would be many more before the evening was over. He wasn't going to rush it, he needed to wait.

"Hey man, looks like you are smitten badly." Mark nodded towards Inga.

"What? She seems nice."

"Seems like you can't stop looking at her."

"Just trying to keep track of her. She did promise me a dance." Erik continued staring at Inga.

"Since you basically just met her, you might want to settle it down a little. Women don't like to go fast. At least not until they get to know you."

"I haven't done anything yet."

"Exactly, so slow down a little. Take your time."

"I'm just going to dance with her. And then..."

"She just looked this way," Mark informed Erik.

"And then, I'm going to ask her out to dinner."

"You're not going to get so wrapped up in the mood after the dance and kiss her, are you?" Mark asked.

"Of course, not. Why? Is that how it's done in America?"

"No. The chances of getting slapped or never seeing her again would have a high probability after that."

"Got it. No kissing. At least not tonight," Erik agreed.

Erik took a swig of his ale and focused on the band. Inga just happened to be in his line of view. The bar was now crowded with Viking clad patrons singing along to the songs while downing their drinks.

Towards the end of the first set, Erik made his way through the crowd to where Inga was standing. "Care to dance?" Erik extended his hand to Inga.

She laughed. "I thought you'd never ask."

"Just waiting for the right song."

"I'd love to." Inga took his hand and followed him to the dance floor.

Smooth blues orchestrated throughout the patio as the acoustic guitar hummed sweetly in harmony with the horns. Their bodies moved in unison with the music. After the song ended, they stood waiting in anticipation for the next song. The soul searing Helvegen song came next.

Erik moved behind Inga, wanting to wrap his arms around her waist but knew it was a temptation he needed to resist at least for now, as they listened to the Viking funeral song. After the music stopped, he graciously walked her back to the sound booth.

He wanted nothing more at that moment than to kiss her. It was ultimately bad timing completely and he knew it was best left for a later and better time. "That was an outstanding version of Helvegen. What did you think?" he asked.

"To be perfectly honest, it's the only version I've heard besides Wardruna's. But yes, I thought it was excellent and very moving."

"Would you be interested in having dinner sometime with me, preferably somewhere quieter where we could have a conversation?"

"I'd love to." Inga stepped into the sound booth and reached into her purse to get one of her business cards. "Here is my card. I look forward to hearing from you."

Erik nodded. "I'll be in touch." He walked back to a high-top table where Mark was standing, sipping his ale.

"Card in hand. Good job." Mark gave him a thumbs up gesture.

"Thanks." He looked at the card she handed to him. Unique Events was the company where she worked. For some strange reason the name sounded familiar, but he couldn't recall why. It had been a long day and he'd had a few of his company's ales. Perhaps tomorrow, it would come to him.

He chanced a look back towards the sound booth, but it was empty. "How long do I have to wait to call her?"

Mark grinned. "Not tonight, for sure. Better wait until Sunday at least."

"Never felt like this about a woman before. It just feels like I should be with her."

"You got it really bad. Sure hope she feels the same way about you." Mark finished up his ale. "I saw her leave. You ready to head out?"

"No reason to stay, unless you have your eye on someone you need to talk to?"

Mark shook his head and they walked toward the exit.

CHAPTER 7

Inga spent the next morning and the next day thinking about Erik. Her attraction to him was so strong, but she couldn't understand why. There was no denying he was one extremely good-looking guy, but she knew nothing about him. Relief had spread through her tense body when he'd asked for permission to call her. Dinner would be a perfect opportunity to learn about each other's history, including what they liked and didn't like.

Sunday evening her phone rang and the caller was unknown. Generally, she didn't pick up calls from numbers she didn't recognize, but she'd been patiently, or so she'd convinced herself, waiting for a call from Erik and she didn't know his number. So, she tapped her phone to answer the call.

"Hello." She waited for a response.

"It's Erik. How was the rest of your weekend?"

"Great. Just catching up on some projects and running errands."

"We talked about having dinner, so I'm calling to see how your week looks. Would Thursday night work for you?"

"Thursday should be okay. Where would you like me to meet you?" Inga asked.

"It's supposed to be good weather Thursday, so I was thinking

Maynard's on the lake in Excelsior would be nice. They have a nice outdoor patio. Should we say six thirty?"

"I'll be there. I look forward to seeing you again."

"Great. I'll see you there," Erik agreed.

Inga hung up the phone and did her happy dance. She was more than excited to see Erik again, and was looking forward to getting to know him better.

Monday morning came way too soon as the weekends went by extremely quick. She arrived at the office at eight-thirty.

Karoline popped her head through Inga's office door opening. "Don't forget we have the brewery meeting at ten."

"You never did mention the name of Olav's cousin's brewery."

"Nordic Brewery. We should leave in an hour." Karoline shut the door and walked down the hall to her office.

At nine sharp, they walked into the lobby of Nordic Brewing.

For the past hour, Inga had been trying to sort out the whole Erik, Nordic Brewing and Olav's cousin thing in her mind. Was the Erik she'd met actually Olav's cousin who owned Nordic Brewing? It was totally possible. She hadn't said anything to Karoline about Erik because she'd sworn off men only a week or so ago.

"Can I help you?" the receptionist asked.

"I'm Karoline and this is Inga and we're with Unique Events."

"Great. I'll let Mr. Johansen know you're here."

Inga watched the receptionist walk into an office down the hallway. Her eyes were glued to the now empty hallway.

"He'll be right with you." The receptionist returned to her desk.

Although, it was certainly unexpected a few hours ago that she would be meeting Erik, it was now expected. Her expectations were met when Erik entered the hall from what most likely was his office. His attire, a modern styled suit complete with the jacket, clean shaven face and a side angled grin met her surprised face.

"Hello, nice to meet you, Karoline and Inga. I'm Erik Johansen. Please join me in the conference room and we can discuss your needs for the Halloween event."

Inga followed Karoline into the spacious room, but she didn't miss his swift perusal of her. Suddenly, she was acutely aware of her chosen attire for the day. Somehow, the quickly thrown together outfit wasn't quite fitting what she would've chosen for her next meeting with Erik. The dress black ankle pants and turquoise blouse portrayed a business professional look which was what she was aiming for, it just wasn't in the sexy category.

She took a seat across the table from Erik, and Karoline sat down beside her.

"It's so nice to meet you, Karoline. And it's a pleasure to see you again, Inga."

Karoline's bewildered look wasn't missed by Inga or Erik.

"I had the pleasure of serving you a Viking Blonde Ale at the James J. Hill Days event a couple of weeks ago." Erik looked toward Inga trying to cover his apparent blunder.

"Yes."

"I'm assuming you liked our newest ale since you are here to discuss serving it at your Halloween event."

Karoline sat quietly watching the interesting exchange between Inga and Erik. "Actually, Olav highly recommended your company, which is why we are here."

"Yes, he mentioned that when he set up this appointment."

Inga handed him a folder with the layout and schedule for the event. "The name of the event is *Skol on All Hallow's Eve*, so the theme is Vikings."

"I like it. Will there be costumes?"

"We certainly hope so." Karoline smiled at him.

"Will you be wearing a costume?" Erik directed his question to Inga.

"I'm hoping to."

Erik studied the event proposal in front of him. "I think our Nordic Ales would fit nicely with your event. I'm assuming this is outside. Do we provide our own tent or do you have tents for the vendors?"

"We can provide a tent or you can. Whichever you prefer," Karoline added to the conversation.

"I think our tent would work the best for your event. Since it is Viking themed, you will like the Vikings portrayed on our event tent."

"Great. The contract is in the file." Karoline motioned toward the table.

Erik read over the contract, signed it and handed it to Karoline. "I look forward to working with your company. It should be a great event with everything you have lined up." He stood up and moved toward the door, opening it for Inga and Karoline who had also stood up to leave.

He walked them to the front door. "I'll be in touch," Erik said shaking Karoline's hand. He reached over to shake Inga's hand and that strange tingling sensation flowed through their bodies.

Inga abruptly pulled her hand back and followed Karoline out the door to their car.

What the heck was going on! This whole weird sensation thing was driving her crazy. She definitely needed to make a doctor's appointment to find out what was causing it. Realizing he wasn't going to acknowledge their other meeting, she felt herself relax. Just a bit, anyway. Probably only for a few minutes though, as she was sure Karoline had a few questions of her own.

"What was that all about?" Karoline shut her car door and turned toward Inga.

Inga slowly sat down in the passenger seat. "I don't know what you're talking about. Just what are you asking?"

"Let me say this in plain English. Why didn't you tell me you met Erik before today?"

"The first time or the second time? You really need to keep up."

"I feel hurt that you didn't tell me about meeting him. Both times. After all, we are best friends, right?"

"Of course we are. The first time was nothing. He was in the Nordic Brewing booth and served me a beer at the James J. Hill Days event in Wayzata. Remember, it was my book club night and we decided to walk around to enjoy the event instead of having a meeting in the bookstore."

"I remember."

"I'd just sworn off men. Remember that, too? So just because some hot guy served me a beer, or I guess *ale* is the correct word, there wasn't anything to tell."

"Okay, so let's move on to the second time, one that neither of you acknowledged in the meeting we just had." Karoline started the engine and pulled out of the parking lot onto the main road.

"I went to the listen to the band on Friday night after work at the Valhalla Nordic Smoke and Ale House. Erik was there, dressed as a Viking. He recognized me from the Wayzata event and introduced himself. That's the first time I found out his name. We danced and he invited me to dinner, so I gave him my business card."

"And?" Karoline coaxed for more information.

"He called on Sunday night and we're having dinner on Thursday night to get to know each other."

"Yes! That's great! Erik is a genuinely nice guy according to Olav. I approve."

"I was going to tell you about meeting him today after our morning appointment. I had no idea Erik was Olav's cousin *or* that he owned Nordic Brewing," Inga stated.

"He was probably just being a gentleman and since you didn't bring up meeting him by accident at Valhalla Nordic Smoke and Ale House, he didn't either. I'm not sure Erik would've recognized the company name on your business card. I'm sure Olav just told him I'd be stopping by with a colleague this morning with a business proposal for him. This is so exciting! I saw the way he looked at you, this just may be the one. I have this strange feeling that he might be your true soul mate." A huge grin spread across Karoline's face.

"Great. Don't go getting us married off already, we haven't even had our first date or first kiss yet."

"Keep your heart open, Inga. You just never know what will happen."

"I have to be honest, he's one really good-looking guy who seems to have a lot going for him, but..."

"But what?" Karoline pulled into the parking lot of their Unique Events office.

"He still lives in Norway, right?"

"Yes, but that doesn't mean he won't move here for the right incentive. Like falling in love. After all, he just started up a company here, didn't he?"

"We'll see what happens. But right now, we have to finish up all the loose ends for the event. And nothing will happen with Erik until our date on Thursday."

Inga got out of the car and headed into the office to get to work. She needed to stop thinking about Erik and focus on her job. Unfortunately, all she could think about was Erik and how drawn she was to him. About how badly she wanted him to kiss her. Damn! Now she was even fantasizing about the man. She needed to stop thinking about him and the affect he had on her.

CHAPTER 8

F ocusing on the Halloween event had been her primary
concern for the week. Finally, Thursday arrived and her
anxiety level was high. Why did she feel so nervous about a
date? She had no idea. She'd spent hours deciding what to wear
because she wanted to look her best for him. Heck, she didn't even
really know the man or what type of woman he liked. Just because he
looked good didn't mean they had anything in common. But to say
the least, she really hoped they had a lot of things in common, because
she really wanted a second date. Even a third and so on. But most of
all she wanted to fall in love, get married and stay married for a good
fifty years, like her parents. All she needed to do was find the right
guy, the one who wanted the same things in life and wanted her by his
side. She'd desired these things for a long time, but hadn't had any
luck in attaining either of them.

Inga finally decided on a casual business type dress that fit her
body like a glove. The teal color brought out the blue in her aqua blue
eyes. A pair of black pumps and a black fitted hip-length jacket
completed the outfit nicely. She was surely dressing to impress.

Eager to see him again, she pulled up to Maynard's with about ten
minutes to spare and found a parking spot. The Minneapolis area had

been blessed with *Indian Summer* weather including temps in the mid-seventies. While she walked to the door, she saw Erik waiting with his blond hair blowing in the light breeze. It was his high cheek boned face, sporting a summer tan, and piercing blue eyes that had attracted her to him the instant she'd seen him at the James J. Hill Days event. Today, his pristine attire, black dress pants with a brown and black striped shirt only made his appearance more attractive to her. She liked a guy who dressed fashionably.

He smiled at her when their eyes met. "It's so good to see you again, Inga." He held the door open and they walked inside.

"I have your table ready, sir. This way." The hostess led them to a table overlooking the lake where they sat down. "Your waiter is Steven and he'll by right with you."

"Thanks," Erik replied.

The hostess left and they opened their menus.

"Hi, I'm Steven and I'll be your waiter this evening. Can I get you something to drink?"

"I'll have a Viking Blonde Ale. What would you like Inga?"

"I'll have one, too."

The waiter nodded and left the table.

"It's good to see you again. Thank you for joining me, so we can talk and get to know each other."

"This atmosphere makes it a bit easier to carry on a conversation than the bar."

"Olav told me you filled Karoline in on our meeting at the Valhalla Nordic Smoke and Ale House. I didn't say anything that morning since you didn't mention it."

"Yes, thanks for that. I didn't have a chance to talk to Karoline about it before our meeting."

"You're welcome."

The waiter reappeared with their ale. "Are you ready to order?"

"I'll try your Norwegian Salmon dinner," Erik said.

"I'll have the Cod special," Inga said.

The waiter disappeared with the order.

"How long have you and Karoline had your company?" Erik asked.

"We went to college together at Augsburg University in Minneapolis. After graduation, we both worked for different companies planning events for about five years before we decided to start our own company together. We've owned the business now for about three years."

"Sounds like you and Karoline are pretty close."

"Oh, yes. We're best friends. I forgot to mention we went to high school together, too."

"Do you approve of Olav?"

"They make a perfect couple. How about you? What's your story?"

"Born and raised in Norway, near Bergen. I started a brewing company in my mid-twenties after working in a few different breweries. By the time I was thirty, we were exporting to other countries and needed to build a larger facility. We wanted to get into the U.S. market, but I decided I wanted to open a smaller version of the brewery in the U.S. first to see how it goes. The shipping costs are so high that it made more sense to brew the ale here and then distribute it in the U.S."

"Wow. Quite the entrepreneur. Is it difficult to do business here since I'm assuming you are a Norwegian citizen not a U.S. citizen?"

"Actually, my mother was a U.S. citizen, born and raised in Wisconsin. She met my dad when she was accepted into a student exchange program in Norway while she was in high school. When one parent is a Norwegian citizen and one is a U.S. citizen, the children are allowed dual citizenship. So, to answer your question, I am a U.S. citizen. And a Norwegian citizen. Kinda the best of both worlds."

"No wonder your English is flawless."

"My mother taught us when we were young."

"But have you ever lived here before?"

"No, but we visited my grandparents in Wisconsin every year. It was a promise my father made to my mother to get her to move to Norway permanently."

"So, no wife or girlfriend back in Norway?"

Erik grinned. "You are direct. I like that. No girlfriend or wife. I was too busy building my company and gone a lot of the time since I ended up doing a lot of traveling to promote the business. Ultimately, I never took the time to get involved with anyone. How about you? You're a very beautiful woman. I don't see a ring and I know Americans are big on them, but a boyfriend?"

"No boyfriend or husband." Inga was extremely glad to know they were both unattached.

"Good." He smiled.

The waiter brought their salads and rolls, so they began eating and soon the main entrees arrived.

The dinner conversation centered on much lighter subjects.

"Living in Minnesota, do you ski?" Erik asked.

"Yes, I learned when I was little. We get a lot of snow in the winter, so we have a few ski hills in town and more up in northern Minnesota."

"We learn as children, also. Only we have mountains instead of hills. I've heard that Minnesota has skiing, but I've always wanted to ski in Colorado."

"I've skied Vail, Breckenridge and Steamboat. The mountain snow is different than ours. Much fluffier. Not that ours isn't good, but it tends to get so cold here most winters that you don't even want to venture out. At least not when it's negative twenty degrees outside."

"Can't wait for that! But the summers are good I hear."

"The best. Of course, when you have more than ten thousand lakes, what more could you want?" Inga teased.

"Besides a fjord?"

They laughed and finished their meals then took a walk outside to the lake.

"I had a lovely dinner. The company was above average." Inga smiled.

"Me, too. I'd like to see more of you. Besides at the Halloween event, where we'll both be busy working," Erik teased.

"I think that can be arranged."

They walked to the parking lot. She got in her car and put the window down since he was still standing beside her door.

"I'll call you." Erik smiled and walked away.

CHAPTER 9

Inga was in love. She knew it was too soon, and she always fell hard and fast, but the feelings were so intense this time. Never had she felt this way before. It was almost as if something was pulling her to him. Being with him seemed so natural, like it was meant to be. She had such a good feeling about Erik. But hadn't she promised herself to take it slow this time? She would try, but he could definitely be *The One* for her.

After she arrived home, she called Karoline.

"Well, how did it go?" Karoline asked.

"It was good. Very good. Can I keep him?" Inga laughed.

"Guess that's up to him. And you. Are you going out again?"

"He'll call. I'm sure of it."

"This sounds promising. I'm happy for you. No red flags came up?" Karoline asked.

"Only that he lives in Norway."

"Well, I'm sure if he opened Nordic Brewing in Minneapolis, he'll be spending time here."

"I have some things to do, before bed, so I'm going to get going. I'll see you in the morning."

The next day was crazy busy and entirely spent on getting everything ready for the *Ladies Night Out* event in Excelsior on Friday. Typically, these types of events were held on a week night, but some people thought the turn outs were low due to it being a work night. So, Friday night was something new and they were holding it from four to seven. A large tent for vendors was put up at the end of Main Street near Lake Minnetonka. The streets were closed in the downtown area and leading to, but not in front of, Maynard's restaurant. The downtown shops were all offering specials and staying open until seven.

The large tent would be filled with vendors selling jewelry, clothing, facial products, hair products, household items, travel companies and a few food vendors including wine. A second tent would be filled with tables and chairs to sit down and relax while listening to music provided by a local female singer and her band.

Inga and Karoline arrived in Excelsior around ten in the morning on Friday. The streets had been blocked off the night before. Tents were already set up in the assigned locations including the tables and chairs. Vendors would be arriving at noon since set up was from noon to two. Time flew by and soon the ladies began arriving. In a flash, the streets and tents were filled with ladies, both young and old, eager to shop and enjoy some food and wine.

Before they knew it, it was seven and the stores along with the vendors closed up their shops. The ladies either headed home or to one of the local bars and restaurants to extend their evening. Promptly at eight, the trucks rolled in to load the tents and chairs, along with the city trucks to pick up the road closure signs.

"I think our first Friday night *Ladies Night Out* was a success," Karoline said as she sat down on a street bench next to Inga and stretched her legs out.

"I agree. It sure does feel good to sit down, though."

"Want to grab something to eat at Maynard's? Olav just sent me a text that he and Erik are there and would love it if we joined them."

Inga's face lit up. "Of course, I do. Let's go."

"Can't we sit a little bit longer?"

Inga jumped up and grabbed Karoline's hand. "We can sit when we get there."

"Well, aren't we full of energy all of a sudden. Could it be because of Erik?" Karoline teased.

"Whatever! Quit walking so slow!" Inga said as she coaxed an exhausted Karoline to walk faster toward the restaurant.

The sun was just setting as they walked down the street. Red streaks filled the horizon with a glorious sunset over Lake Minnetonka.

"This way." Karoline pulled Inga toward the outside entrance to the deck area by the lake. "Olav texted me that they are outside on the deck next to a bonfire."

The deck was filled with people, actually mostly women from the *Ladies Night Out* event, but they quickly spotted Olav and Erik at a table by a fire pit. Multiple outside heaters dotted the deck to keep the patrons warm as the temperature dropped to the fifties.

"Glad you ladies could join us. Take a seat. I even brought a couple of blankets per Karoline's request. Did you know in Oslo, the restaurants and bars provide blankets for the customers?" Olav stated.

"Really. Maybe we should suggest it to Maynard's and start a new custom here," Karoline suggested.

"It's becoming quite the rage. I even saw them in some restaurants in Ålesund recently," Erik added.

Karoline and Inga sat down at the table, unfolding the blankets and placing them over their laps.

"How was your event?" Erik asked totally focused on Inga.

"It was great! We had a record turnout. About 500 more than they had last year," Inga replied.

"What would you ladies like to drink?" Olav asked.

Inga noticed they already had what appeared to be beer. "What are you guys drinking?"

"Nordic Brewing's Viking Blonde Ale, of course," Erik stated proudly.

"I should've guessed. Sounds like you're getting your name out there with the local bars," Inga stated.

"We're trying."

"I hate to admit it but I've never tried one of your ales, so I'll have one," Karoline explained.

"Me, too." Inga nodded. "We need to support our friends."

Erik smiled in response, as he got up to get the drinks. "I'll get them."

"Hey, you ladies hungry?" Olav asked.

"We were so busy we never had a chance to have dinner. What are they serving outdoors?" Karoline asked.

Olav handed them the menus. "It's just hamburgers and sandwiches, if that's okay?"

"A hamburger sounds good to me," Karoline said.

"I'm going to have a grilled chicken sandwich. Do we go up to the grill shack to order them or do they have waiters?" Inga asked.

Moments later, a waiter walked by and Olav flagged him down, just as Erik returned with the glasses of ale.

The waiter took their orders and left.

"I have to say, this is good, Erik," Karoline said after tasting the Viking Blonde Ale.

"Thanks, glad you like it. Hope lots more people like it and then *'we're in business'* as they say."

Their food came out quickly and they ate while listening to the band play. It definitely wasn't Viking music but the band did a nice job playing cover songs from the eighties and nineties. Including Prince, since he was considered a local in Minnetonka, having owned a house on nearby Christmas Lake. Soon it was eleven, and since it had been such a long day, they all decided to call it a day.

"I can give Karoline a ride, then you won't have to drive her home," Olav offered.

"That sounds great, I'm tired," Inga answered.

"Where are you parked? Let me walk you to your car, so you don't have to walk alone," Erik offered.

"Thanks for asking, I'd appreciate it. I don't like walking into parking lots alone this late at night."

Olav and Karoline walked toward the over flow parking lot for

Maynard's restaurant as Inga and Erik walked back to the main street parking lot where Inga's car was parked.

Inga unlocked the door and opened it. Standing between the door and the car, she anticipated what it would be like to be kissed by Erik. After all, he was only standing inches from her. Her desire to be kissed by him was so intense, she could hardly stand it.

"I'm glad you joined us at Maynard's this evening. It was unplanned but extremely enjoyable. I *will* give you a call, next week." He grinned at her.

Erik's sexy grin almost completely undid her to the point of pulling his face toward hers and planting a big kiss on his lips. *What was stopping him?* Dang, she was trying to go too fast again, and he was doing the right thing by taking it slow. Since she could feel the chemistry, she was sure he could. He just had far more control than she did.

She watched as he walked away, then slowly sat down in her car and drove home. There was always next time. At least, she hoped there would be a next time.

CHAPTER 10

I nga wasn't sure sleep would come easy even though she hit the bed fast and hard. She'd scrubbed her make-up off gently, shed her clothes, and slipped into her pajamas quickly as she was running totally on empty. It had been a long day with an exciting evening full of intense longing for a man she'd only just met recently. Her eyes closed as soon as her head landed on the pillow, while visions of being kissed by Erik filled her thoughts before she fell asleep.

The alarm went off at eight and she immediately reached for the off button. Saturday and Sunday were her only days to sleep in, and oh how she loved sleeping late especially after a long and tiring evening. First thing on her agenda was cleaning her townhouse, next she was off to run errands and get her nails done. She was meeting her friend, Jackie, later for dinner and wine. Most likely, later in the itinerary, there would be some chocolate involved. Maybe, if she kept busy, she could stop thinking about Erik.

Later that day, she arrived just before seven at the Victoria Jazz Club in the quaint town of Victoria to meet Jackie. They were trying out the club's seafood salad and checking out the Dakota Jazz group.

Unique Events was always putting on events where they needed music. Nice smooth tones that welcomed conversations. Subsequently many of her weekends were spent checking out the food produced by local chefs and on the lookout for new bands to complement their events.

"So, how's my 'check out new music' partner?" Jackie walked up and gave Inga a hug.

"Great. How 'bout you?"

"About as exciting as retail fashion can be! But we have all our new fall fashions out and all the summer clothing is on clearance."

"I'll have to stop by and see if I can find any good deals to my liking."

Inga and Jackie walked into the club to find a table.

"I'm really excited to try their new seafood salad. I heard it has good old Minnesota walleye in it." Inga picked up the menu and spotted it under specials.

"Oh, look. They also have Walleye Gumbo," Jackie announced.

"That sounds good, too. I may need to have both."

Shortly after they ordered, the band, Dakota Jazz, started their first set. Inga and Jackie sat back in their chairs to enjoy the smooth jazz music surrounding them. Their glasses of MN Blushing Bride, a local sweet blush wine, from the Next Chapter Winery in New Prague arrived before the first song ended. Dinner would be served at the first intermission as to not interrupt any of the patron's listening pleasure.

"This is really good wine. Have you ever been to their winery?" Inga asked.

"No, but I think we should put them on our list of places to visit," Jackie stated.

"I'll have to check them out to see if they are interested in having us plan any events for them. I always prefer doing business with companies that I'd personally recommend their products."

As soon as the first set ended, the wait staff promptly brought out the dinner plates.

Inga took her first spoonful of the soup and fell in love. "This is unbelievably superb. The broth is thick but smooth, filled with appropriate spices and an ample supply of walleye chunks."

Jackie had ordered the same. They decided on the Minnesota soup and sandwich special consisting of a walleye seafood salad served on a piece of wild rice bread and accompanied with a cup of walleye gumbo soup.

"Anyone who likes seafood salads will love this. The flavor is impeccable and bursting with the walleye," Jackie said after tasting a bite.

"I think they definitely have a winner on their hands."

The tables were cleared quickly after they finished eating and the band began their second set.

Inga and Jackie left around eleven and walked to their cars in the parking lot.

"That was fun," Inga said. "Can't wait to see what you come up with next. Good job on finding something new and different."

"Just trying to help my friend with ideas for her 'Unique Events'." Jackie laughed.

They hugged, then got into their cars to head home.

Inga was thankful to Jackie for spending the evening with her, so she could stop thinking about Erik. But right now, she couldn't help wondering if he drank wine or only ale and if he'd ever tried good old-fashioned Minnesota walleye. She was pretty sure they didn't have walleye in Norway, but wasn't certain of it. Whenever fish was mentioned as far as Norway was concerned, she'd only heard Lutefisk talked about which, of course, was actually a cod fish. As for her, she'd never tried Lutefisk. Every fall there were numerous Lutefisk dinners held in the Twin Cities. She'd seen them advertised in the local city newspapers, but it had been years since she'd gone to one. They usually started in October and were held at various Lutheran churches all over Minnesota up until Christmas, at least that's what she'd heard.

Maybe it was time she attended one again, since 'Unique Events' were her specialty and Lutefisk was definitely unique. She was sure Jackie would be game to go, but perhaps she could invite Erik?

Inga fell asleep thinking about a strangely unique food —Lutefisk!

～

Sunday morning, Inga woke to a cloud filled sky. She dressed for church and was out the door within the hour. Her prayer for the day focused on asking for God's help to take her new relationship slow and of course to let Erik be 'the one' for her.

Later that afternoon at her townhouse, she decided to turn on the fireplace, chill out on the couch and get caught up on some of her favorite shows by doing a little bit of binge watching. A nice autumn themed Hallmark movie would certainly work. After a couple hours, she dozed off and woke to her phone ringing.

"Hello," she said without looking to see who was calling.

"Hi, it's Erik. Is this a good time?"

"Perfect." Inga rubbed her eyes to wake up faster, if that was even possible, after she heard his name and shifted upward to a sitting position on the couch.

"How was your weekend?"

"I spent Saturday night with my friend, Jackie. We had dinner at a jazz club and listened to some great music."

"Sounds fun."

"How about you? How was your weekend?"

"Busy. I was manning our booth at the Red Wing Arts Festival. We were lucky and the rain held off which resulted in a good turnout. It seems like more men attend the art festivals and generally they like our ale, so we served a fair amount of our signature—Viking Blonde Ale."

"It sounds like your Nordic Brewery is off to a great start. Art fairs are always fun and present an eclectic group of attendees," Inga offered.

"I would've asked you to come along, but I had to work the booth. Maybe next year, I'll be more established and can have someone else take over that duty."

"Sounds like a plan. You know I'm going to put that date on my calendar." Inga laughed.

"Speaking of plans, would you like to have dinner one night this week?"

"I think I could squeeze in dinner. How about Thursday or Friday night?"

"Friday works. I can pick you up or we can meet somewhere after work, whichever you'd prefer," Erik offered.

"If you want to pick me up at my townhouse in Eden Prairie at six, we can pick a nearby restaurant."

"That will work. See you Friday."

"Great. See you then." Inga heard the click of the phone meaning he'd disconnected the call. She set her phone down, stood up and did her happy dance around the living room floor while her heart threatened to leap out of her chest. She couldn't wait to see Erik again. This was definitely going to be the start of 'Erik and Inga' and hopefully a long lasting and loving relationship.

CHAPTER 11

Erik strolled into Willy McCoy's in Bloomington to join Olav for a burger and beer. The Minnesota Vikings would be playing football at seven and all the TV screens were tuned to the game channel.

He immediately spotted Olav at the bar and took the seat next to him. "How's it going?"

"Good, cousin. This should be a great game tonight since they seem to be on top of their game finally and on a winning streak."

Erik shook his head and laughed. "Still trying to wrap my head around American Football. It's so different than European Football. Your guys don't generally kick the ball, in fact for the most part, they throw it or carry it."

"I get what you're saying. But it is what it is."

"Exactly. So, I'm trying to learn all the rules for your game, since it seems to be the thing to do in Minnesota. Although, I have to say I'm all for the name of your team, Vikings!"

"Compliments your latest offering, Viking Blonde Ale, very nicely," Olav said holding up his glass. "Skol!"

Erik picked up his glass and they both drank to the toast.

They watched the kick off and cheered each time the Vikings scored. During a commercial the conversation turned toward women.

"Karoline, mentioned you and Inga have been talking," Olav stated.

"Inga?"

"Yah, Inga."

"She's very nice." Erik smiled.

"I know, but you said you weren't going to be staying permanently in the U.S. And you weren't going to get involved with anyone because of just that fact."

"I'm not involved with anyone."

"Yet, but where is this thing with Inga going?" Olav asked.

"We just met."

"Karoline and I are getting along very well. We are probably heading for a serious relationship. I really like her a lot."

"That's good. I'm happy for you. Not sure what that has to do with my relationship with Inga?"

"Since you are going back to Norway in maybe less than a year, and you said you're not going to have a serious relationship with anyone here, where does that leave Inga?"

"We can be friends, can't we? Or are American women different?"

"I don't think Karoline or Inga would approve of your definition of friends, which we both know means friends with benefits."

"Isn't that done in America?"

"I suppose. But Inga is looking for a long term, permanent relationship."

"And Karoline?"

"Yes, her too. But I'm planning on staying in the U.S."

"Do you think Inga would come to Norway?" Erik asked.

"Probably to visit, but not to live. She's American and this is her home."

"So far, we've only gone on one date. I like her and I think we would get along well. And besides that, she's gorgeous. She has Norwegian ancestry. Did you know that?"

"Yes, Karoline mentioned it," Olav answered.

"We haven't even kissed, yet. So, I think this is all a bit premature."

"Maybe. But I want you keep this conversation in mind, going forward. If you break Inga's heart, it will be on me. Karoline will blame me for introducing you two."

"Actually, we met before the day at Nordic Brewing. We sort of met at James J. Hill Days. We probably would've met again even if you hadn't set up the meeting, but who knows, we might not have."

"You didn't mention that," Olav said.

She stopped at our tent to buy a beer and left immediately to catch up with her friends who'd kept walking. At least, it appeared that way. That's it, nothing more. Didn't have any idea who she was and didn't even get her name."

"I didn't know."

"I'll see how it goes. But it might not be up to any of us. It just might be fate which is something none of us have control over."

"I hope you're right," Olav said and took a drink of his ale. He returned his focus to the game on the big screen.

Erik stared up at the screen, but his thoughts were on Inga. He liked her a lot more than he'd anticipated. He'd promised himself before he left Norway that he wouldn't get involved with anyone in America. Primarily because of the predicament he now found himself in. He felt so drawn to her that he wasn't sure he could end it before it even started. Hell, he wanted to kiss her with a feeling so intense, he felt the desire throughout every inch of his body. He'd never felt like this with any woman before.

He was planning on kissing her on their upcoming date on Friday, even if it was just a kiss goodnight. Maybe, it would be just a mediocre kiss or not a good kiss at all. Then all his troubles would be over.

But what if the kiss was earth-shattering and the best he'd ever experienced? He had a gut feeling it would be great and he would end up having a whole lot of soul searching to do afterwards. It may come down to the decision of a lifetime for him, when the time came, to consider whether to have a relationship with Inga or to walk away.

The bar filled with screams as the Vikings scored another touchdown. Erik looked up at the screen above the bar and tried to change his focus to the game.

CHAPTER 12

Monday was busy as usual and Inga had already left a message for someone from the Next Chapter Winery to contact her. She really wanted to do business with them in the future and was eager to visit their vineyard. Lately, she'd read in the paper that wineries with their own vineyards were popping up in Minnesota. Who'd have thought grapes would grow well in the colder climate to the extent that it could be profitable? Heck, she was all for entrepreneurship.

An hour later, her phone rang.

"Hello, this is Inga."

"Hi, I'm Sara with Next Chapter Winery and I'm returning your call."

"Thank you, I was just introduced to your MN Blushing Bride wine and loved it. My company is Unique Events and we are interested in possibly coordinating some events with your winery. You can look us up on our website, www.unique.events.com. Perhaps I can stop by when it's convenient for you and we could discuss possible opportunities that could benefit both of our companies?"

"We are always open to discussing new marketing ideas. Let me check out your website and talk to the other owners. If it's something they'd be interested in, I'll call you back to set up a meeting day and time."

"Great, I look forward to hearing from you."

Inga wasn't too sure about the phone conversation, but she knew Unique Events had a fabulous website and it would do great job of selling their company.

Inga walked into Karoline's office and handed her a menu from the Victoria Jazz Club. "Jackie and I checked this place out on Saturday night. The 'Walleye Salad Sandwich and Walleye Gumbo Soup Combo' was unbelievably delicious. We need to use them for an event."

"That good, huh? Lucky for you, I see on the back of the brochure that they offer catering!"

"Oh, and we sampled some wine from a local vineyard, Next Chapter Winery in New Prague. And get this, the name of the wine was MN Blushing Bride!"

"Wow. Sounds like you and Jackie had a great night."

"What more can you ask for? Great food, wine and the band was pretty good, too."

"Sorry, I missed it."

"Bet you are! How was your date with Olav?" Inga asked.

"I really like him. He's so great. We always have a good time together."

"Is this thing with you two getting serious?"

"I think it is. We are spending a whole lot of time together. He's a really good kisser, too." Karoline couldn't stop the huge smile spreading across her face.

"Well, that explains everything." Inga laughed.

"Speaking of guys, have you heard from Erik?"

"Yes, he's picking me up at my townhouse on Friday night and we're going to have dinner."

"I hope you don't like him too much," Karoline stated matter-of-factly.

"What's that supposed to mean?" Inga felt surprised by the statement.

"Oh, I don't know. I just don't want you to get your heart broken again."

"I'll be careful. I'm trying to go slow. It probably helps that we are both so busy with our jobs."

"Just keep in mind your concerns about him going back to Norway to live."

"I am. Speaking of Olav being a good kisser, Erik hasn't kissed me yet. Don't you think it's about time he did? After all, that could be the deal breaker. You know how much I like guys who excel in kissing."

"Well, it's important, but living in Norway will probably be the deal breaker. And it's about time you dated a guy who wasn't in such a hurry. Take your time and get to know him first."

Inga's phone rang. She glanced at it to see who was calling. "Oh, I put a call in to the winery so we can set up a meeting. This is them." Inga tapped the phone as she walked out of Karoline's office to hers, "This is Inga."

"This is Sara, from Next Chapter Winery. Would you be able to stop in tomorrow at eleven?"

"Yes, I can make that. I look forward to meeting you and seeing your winery."

"Me, too. See you tomorrow."

Inga ran back to Karoline's office. "They want to meet us tomorrow. This could be a vital contact for us." Inga did her happy dance for just a minute, then straightened into perfect posture to do her professional pose.

"I can't wait to taste some of their wine, since you seem to be quite dazzled by it."

The next morning, Inga and Karoline drove out to New Prague for their meeting at the winery. Unfortunately, the clouds rolled in providing an overcast gloomy kind of day. Inside the car, however, sat two very happy passengers taking in the scenery consisting of

Minnesota farmlands freshly harvested in preparation for the coming winter.

They always tended to allow extra time to make a stop at a local coffee shop or bakery or both. The longtime and well-known Schumacher Inn had closed but the bakery was still open. Inga was counting on them having their famous kolache breakfast pastry buns which were filled with various fruits. Her favorite kolaches were the ones filled with prunes.

Immediately after they opened the door, the sweet aroma of fresh baked rolls filled the air. Inga took a whiff and inhaled deeply. Pleasure washed over her face as she walked straight for the glass display cases showcasing the freshly baked goods for the day.

"I'll take two of the prune kolaches and a bottle of water." Inga pulled out some money and laid it on the counter.

"I'll take two of the raspberry kolaches and a bottle of water." Karoline paid the clerk and they found a table by the window that overlooked the little town's main street.

The clerk brought out their kolaches and they immediately took their first bites savoring the delectable flavor.

"I love this little town. I haven't been out here for ages. I heard they have a small theater producing plays that have received rave reviews." Karoline pointed down the street toward the theater building.

The server wiping the table behind them offered insight into their conversation. "The theater is called 'Daleko Arts' which is a Czech word meaning 'far away' so the name reflects New Prague's strong bohemian roots."

"Thanks. I'm going to have to check out their schedule and come down here to see a show sometime." Inga watched the server walk back behind the counter.

"Maybe, they have a Christmas show we can go to. I'd be interested in going to a show with you," Karoline said.

After they'd finished their treats, they drove down the road to the winery. There was a large arched New Chapter Winery sign marking the entrance roadway. As they followed the road, they passed the vineyard fields and then spotted the main building ahead.

Sara met them at the door and welcomed them into their office building.

"So happy to meet you, Sara," Inga said. "This is Karoline my business partner at Unique Events."

"Nice to meet both of you." Sara shook their hands. "Please follow me and I will show you our vineyards and the winery."

Inga and Karoline followed her as they first entered the winery and then out to the vineyards.

"This is incredible. Up until a few weeks ago, I had no idea Minnesota had vineyards and wineries," Karoline said as they walked along the rows of grapes shaded by their large green leafs.

"It's relatively new to this area, we started this one about eight years ago." Sara led them back to the office.

"Do you have a movable wine bar unit to offer your wine at events?" Inga asked.

"Not yet, but it is something we have discussed. Possibly for next year."

"We set up unique events for our customers and sometimes wine would be the most appropriate beverage to offer. I think we may be able to include you in some of these events, if you'd be interested in doing that?" Inga asked.

"So, you have sampled our wine offerings then?" Sara asked.

"I've only tried your MN Blushing Bride, but fell in love with it immediately." Inga smiled pointing to a bottle of it on the shelf.

"I haven't had the opportunity to sample any of your offerings yet," Karoline said.

"Well, ladies, we need to remedy that. Take a seat at the counter and you can sample our products." Sara walked behind the counter, picked out her favorites and set them on the counter.

Inga and Karoline took seats at the counter.

"This is our MN Dashing Groom. It's a sweet red." Sara poured them a small sampling.

They both nodded their approval.

Sara poured the next one. "This is our Blackberry Delight, a sweet fruit wine."

"I may be strange but I prefer sweet wines and I love this one," Inga said.

"This is our Muscat, it's similar to a Pinot Grigio."

"I love Pinot and this is very good," Karoline said.

"This is our new offering, MN Iced Wine," Sara said as she poured samples.

"Wow! This is incredible. I've never tasted anything like this one before," Inga said.

"The iced wines only started being seen around the 1980's, so to the wine business that is considered new even though they occasionally were produced in the early 1700's in Germany. Only recently have they become popular since more companies are able to produce them. The production for these wines faced difficulties because grapes for *ice wine* must be frozen while on the vine. The sugars and other dissolved solids do not freeze, but the water does, allowing for a more concentrated grape juice to develop, so it is considered a type of dessert wine." Sara put the bottles away.

"These wines would be a hit at our events," Karoline said.

"Let's go back to my office and discuss the business side of offering our wines at your events."

Inga and Karoline left an hour later, feeling very good about their day, along with a bottle of each of the wines they'd tasted.

"I think that was a very productive meeting. It will be good for both companies to do business together. And once they get a trailer fitted for their products, they will be able to do events around the state which will complement their own events held at the winery," Inga said.

"Exactly what I was thinking. I'm glad you sampled that wine last week, otherwise I don't think we'd ever have known about them," Karoline said.

"I'm feeling really good about the samples she gave us. Maybe we need to plan a girl's night at my townhouse with some of our friends?" Inga asked.

"Sounds like an excellent plan. I'm in," Karoline answered.

CHAPTER 13

The next couple of days flew by. Erik emailed her that he was going out of town to attend a Master Brewers Conference in Calgary, Canada, but would be back Friday so he would still be able to make their dinner date that evening. She replied and sent him her address since he would be picking her up at her townhouse.

Thursday was when everything got crazy. It all started with a call from Sara.

"This is Inga."

"This is Sara, from the Next Chapter Winery. I just don't know what to do. Event planning is not my thing and I don't think I can do it."

"Okay, take a deep breath and tell me what's going on."

"We have an event planner, Amy, who handles our wedding bookings at the winery. She's great and everything, but she's pregnant. And she just called and she's at the hospital. The baby came early, by about three weeks. She's fine and baby's fine. I'm not. We have a wedding on Saturday and of course she can't be there now."

"I'm sure everything will be fine. She should have everything set to go by now," Inga offered.

"I'm sure she does but someone has to be here to make sure everything goes as planned. I don't want this bride's wedding to be ruined."

"Isn't there someone else at the winery who could stand in for Amy?"

"No. That's why I'm calling you. Could you do it?"

"Oh."

"We desperately need an event planner to make sure everything goes as planned. We will pay you, of course."

"I'm not familiar with your facility, though. Does Amy have a file with all the info and plans for the wedding?"

"Yes, her husband dropped the file off this morning. I would be able to be here for the wedding with you, if that would help. I just don't know what to do."

"Okay, let me see if Karoline can help. It may be nice to have a couple of people there that night since we are picking it up at the last minute. We would want you there, too, since we don't know our way around your winery yet."

"I can help as long as I don't have to be the one in charge."

"I'll talk it over with Karoline and call you right back." Inga ended the call.

She walked down the hall to Karoline's office. "Want to do a wedding on Saturday?" Inga asked.

"What? Did you say this Saturday? Are you nuts?" Karoline asked.

Inga explained the situation at the winery.

"Of course, we have to help them out. We'll have a client for life and we'll be saving a wedding. And I like weddings." Karoline smiled at Inga.

Inga called Sara back. "Sara. We'll help you with the wedding. We'll stop out at the winery around one this afternoon to go over Amy's plans for this wedding."

"Oh, thank you so much! You are a life saver."

"Have you called the bride yet?"

"No."

"Wait until we get there and we'll call her together after we go over the file. Then we'll know what questions we have for her."

"Okay."

"See you at one."

Inga and Karoline arrived at the winery and took command of the situation. They went over the plans, talked to Amy on the phone, and informed the bride of the change. After a little bit of freaking out by the bride, they had everything under control. They'd made the calls to the pastor, florist, cake, caterer, photographer, videographer and the karaoke company to confirm them for Saturday. They were all fortunate it was an afternoon wedding, which would give them time during the morning to get everything in place. The bride insisted they bring their husbands or boyfriends to the wedding, since they were stepping in to replace the original event planner at the last minute.

On the way back to their office, Inga asked, "Are you going to invite Olav to come to the wedding?"

"I don't know, what do you think? Are you going to ask Erik?"

"It seems like the event is well planned, so assuming nothing else goes wrong, it should go pretty smooth."

"A lot of guys don't like weddings, though."

"It would give them a chance to see us in action."

"I say we ask them," Karoline said.

"Okay," Inga agreed, hoping he would call her tonight about their date tomorrow, so she didn't have to call him.

CHAPTER 14

Inga waited for a phone call from Erik that evening but he didn't call. He was probably busy at the conference, she thought. It was late now, so she would just have to wait until the next morning. She just didn't feel comfortable calling him yet, since they'd only been on one actual date so far.

The next morning was hectic, troubleshooting many last-minute details for the wedding, along with all her other event projects they had on the calendar. Plus, she was really hoping he would call to confirm their evening plans.

Finally, about two he called. "Hi, it's Erik. I'm so sorry but we're going to have to reschedule our date for this evening. My plane out of Calgary is having mechanical issues and we have a three-hour delay. I won't be getting back to Minneapolis until about nine."

"I hate it when that happens. But no one wants to get on a plane that's not working properly."

"Do you have plans for Saturday night?" Erik asked.

"Yes. No. I mean I wanted to talk to you about Saturday night. Karoline and I are filling in at the last minute for a wedding event planner who just had a baby. The baby came early, so they hadn't planned on her being on maternity leave yet. It's at a local winery and the bride is so thankful we will be stepping in to oversee everything for her wedding that she told us to bring husbands or boyfriends along."

"Oh, so you consider me your boyfriend?" Erik laughed.

"Well, I just thought…" Inga began and then stopped.

"I'm flattered. I'd love to go, if that's what you are asking."

"Really?"

"I've never been to a wedding in the U.S. so it would be a new experience."

"Great! Then you can also see us in action doing our event planning stuff."

"Should I assume Karoline is bringing Olav?" he asked.

"Yes."

"What time do you want us to be there? I'm assuming you will be there early to get everything set up ahead of time."

"The wedding is at five."

"I'll talk to Olav and we can drive together. This sounds like it will be a fun night even though they will be serving wine instead of ale." Erik couldn't help laughing.

"Yes, only wine will be served. They have some interesting Minnesota flavors, maybe you'll like one."

"I'm not one of those beer or ale snobs. I do drink wine, too."

"Okay, I'll see you tomorrow night," Inga said.

"I'll still owe you a dinner date, though. We can pick a night later. I'll see you at the wedding." Erik ended the call.

Inga set her phone down and did her now 'Erik' happy dance. That turned out better than she'd expected. He would be at the wedding and she still had a private dinner date with him to look forward to. Now, she could only hope that everything went okay at the wedding. Unique Events had done their fair share of weddings, even some with problems that had come up, but they'd handled them with ease.

Inga headed to Karoline's office. "I just talked to Erik and he has a plane delay in Canada, so we won't be going out to dinner tonight. But we will reschedule."

"I'm sorry."

"And he is going to come to the wedding."

"That's good. Olav will have someone to hang out with while we are working," Karoline said.

"Erik will call him and they can ride together."

"We'll have to coordinate the cars, so I can ride home with Olav and you can ride home with Erik. How about I drive to the wedding and Erik can pick up Olav, so he'll have his car?"

Inga's face lit up. "That works for me!"

That evening since her plans had changed, she decided to see if she could come to a decision on her Halloween costume. She knew she wanted some sort of Viking costume but wasn't sure what she envisioned it looking like. The internet, other than Ebay, would be the best place to look and she needed it soon. On Etsy, she pulled up Viking Valkyrie. She'd become intrigued by the Vikings after watching the History Channel series, Vikings.

Her interest piqued, she looked up the definition of Valkyries online in Wikipedia.

In Norse mythology, a Valkyrie was one of a host of female figures who chose those who died in battle and those who lived. Half of those who died in battle were taken to the afterlife hall of the slain, Valhalla, ruled over by the god Odin. There, the deceased warriors became einherjar who prepared for the events of Ragnarök. The Valkyries served these fallen warriors mead, became lovers of heroes and other mortals, or were sometimes described as the daughters of royalty. They were sometimes accompanied by ravens.

She had to say that she preferred the part of lovers of heroes and daughters of royalty the best. Scrolling down the pages of Etsy under Viking Costumes, she finally found one she thought was closest to what she envisioned. It wasn't a Valkyrie sexy costume but instead a beige Viking era under tunic with a black apron overlaid with silver and gold braided trim that came with silver Celtic designed pins and amber beads. So, for a mere hundred dollars, she placed her order. It would arrive in five days. She was all set, except for a cloak which she might have to do without and hope for warm temps on the event day.

~

Saturday morning at ten-thirty, Karoline arrived to pick her up. It was going to be a long day, but they needed to be at the winery early so they'd be available to look over the cake and flower deliveries for starters. They hoped to have everything set up and ready to go by one at the latest.

Thankfully, when they arrived the chairs were already set up along with the arched challis. Employees were already putting up netting decorations on it and the chairs. At eleven, the flowers arrived. Inga and Sara went over the delivery to make sure they had everything that had been ordered. The florist helped organize the whole order and left an extra box of flowers and corsages in case they were needed.

Karoline was with the caterer helping them get set up in the reception dinner room. The dinner menu was a pasta bar consisting of Fettuccini Alfredo with chicken and spaghetti with meat balls. It also included garlic bread and salad.

The bride's family arrived shortly after noon to set out the table favors and decorate a table with pictures of the bride and groom growing up through the years.

Inga spotted them and walked over to introduce herself. "Hi, I'm Inga."

"I'm Cathy Maxwell the bride's mother."

"It's so nice to meet you," Inga said.

Cathy introduced Inga to a few other people.

"I just want to thank you for stepping in at the last minute to take Amy's place. Have you met my daughter, Lisa, yet?"

"No, is she here now?"

"Yes, follow me and I'll introduce you to her."

Inga followed Cathy into the building where the reception room was located. Off the large dining room was a private bathroom and dressing room for the bridal party to use.

She opened the door after knocking and they walked in. "Lisa, this is Inga with Unique Events," Cathy said.

Inga walked up to shake her hand. "Nice to meet you. How are you holding up?"

"If you tell me you have everything under control, I think I might be able to relax a little bit," Lisa answered.

"Oh, don't you worry about anything," Inga replied. "This is your special day and we have everything falling into place perfectly. The flowers are here, the cake is here and the caterer is unloading and setting up everything for the meal. So, all you need to do is take care of getting yourself into that wedding dress and looking beautiful."

Lisa smiled. "Thank you. Your confidence is making me feel better already."

"I'm going to see how the caterer is doing." Inga slowly left the room, leaving a jittery bride behind her.

"How's it going?" Inga asked Karoline.

"Good. Looks like everything is under control. How's the bride? I saw you go in the bridal party room." Karoline pointed to the room.

"Well, so far, so good. Let's hope it stays that way."

"I checked the outside wedding ceremony area and it looks like everything is set up and decorated. The bad thing is that we weren't in on the whole planning process so we don't know how it's supposed to look. You know how some of these brides get if everything isn't perfect."

"Yes, I know. I'm hoping for no drama tonight. Usually, they relax after the ceremony and in this case, after a couple of glasses of wine," Inga said.

The guests started arriving at four and everyone was seated, including Erik and Olav, by five.

Inga and Karoline waited until the bride walked down the aisle before they took seats in the back row.

The bride was a petite redhead in an ivory full length fitted dress. Her hair was up in ringlets and the flowers were from the autumn colors of the color wheel. Lisa looked absolutely beautiful.

Inga couldn't help hoping that one day in the near future she would be having her own wedding. She glanced over at Erik. He was dressed in a black suit with a baby blue shirt. His blond hair lay perfectly in place. Like she'd said before, he looked like Thor and he was so hot!

Inga straightened her rust colored fitted dress that stopped about mid-thigh. It had a faint pattern in it if you looked closely and a V-neck where her gold locket lay. A gift from her grandmother when she turned sixteen. Her long blonde hair fell in gentle curls. She'd noticed Erik's appreciative gaze and approving nod when she'd sat down and could only hope it meant he liked what he saw.

After the wedding ceremony was over, the guests all made their way to the reception room for a glass of wine to wait for the bride and groom to finish their wedding photo shots. MN Blushing Bride and MN Dashing Groom were the specialty wines being served.

When the couple entered the room, the guests clapped. Finally, the food line was opened and the bride and groom went first, followed by the wedding party, then the guests.

It had been a long day, and Inga and Karoline were the last ones in line, right after Erik and Olav.

Erik turned to greet Inga with a hug. "You look beautiful. How are you holding up?"

"The day is almost over, but thankfully everything went smoothly."

"Did you get a chance to eat yet today?"

"Just a light breakfast, so I'm famished."

They were now at the food table so she filled her plate with the Chicken Alfredo and salad, then took a seat next Erik. She was so pleased that he'd agreed to attend the wedding.

Barely minutes after they started eating, the DJ began playing music for the bride and groom's first dance. Soon the guests filled the dance floor.

"What did you think of the American wedding?" Inga asked.

"It's different than in Norway, but it was a nice wedding. Should I assume that everyone gets married in a vineyard?" Erik laughed.

"No, in fact, most don't. Usually, the ceremony is in a church and the reception is held at a hotel, country club or some other venue."

"Do you want to get married?" Erik asked.

Inga couldn't believe what she'd just heard. "What?"

"Do you ever see yourself getting married?" he clarified.

"Oh, yes. I want to get married and have a family. Just haven't found the right person yet." She hated it when guys asked that question because it always seemed like a trick question. If she answered yes, would they go running for the hills or mountains in Erik's case?

"Me, too." Erik grinned at her. "Would you like to dance?"

"Sure." Inga got up and walked to the dance floor with Erik. The slow song had just ended and a more upbeat song was now playing as they reached the dance floor. After the song was over, they returned to their table to join Karoline and Olav who were deep in conversation.

Sara approached their table. "Inga and Karoline, thank you so much for making sure this wedding went off without a hitch. Everything's been perfect. I think I can take it from here if you want to leave. But if you want to stay, that's perfectly fine, too."

"I think everything went well, but I'm glad you were here to help us." Inga looked at Karoline to see what she was thinking.

"We might stay a little longer and then head out. We can talk more on Monday."

Inga and Karoline stood up and gave Sara a hug before she left the table.

The four picked up their wine glasses and made their way outside to the bonfire.

It was chilly, so Erik took off his suit coat and put it over Inga's shoulders.

"Thank you," Inga said.

"I'm plenty warm, but you looked a little chilly."

Karoline and Olav took a seat on a bench near the fire, but Inga and Erik kept walking and entered the vineyards with the almost full bright moon above them in a clear sky making it almost seem like it was still dusk.

"What are you looking for in the man you want to spend the rest of your life with?" Erik asked when they stopped walking.

"Wow, you are really direct."

"You don't have to answer, if you don't want to."

"I want someone who will get married for life. Who wants children and will be a good father. Who will share his life with me. Who will have common interests with me and mostly who will love me with their whole heart and soul."

"That's a mouthful. But it's good that you know what you want."

"What are you looking for?" she asked.

"I think you brought up all the important things. I have one other thing to add to my list though, and that is they need to be able to and want to travel back and forth between the U.S. and Norway. Both places are my home and I have family in both of them. Do you think that is too much to expect from someone?"

"I don't know. It would be a lot to consider for an American who'd never been to Norway."

"If you and I ended up in a serious relationship, would it be something you would consider doing?"

"I just don't have an answer for that. I've never even been to Norway, so I don't know if I could live there."

"Well, we just might have to take a trip to Norway, so I can show you my beautiful country. If that's something that might interest you?" Erik pulled Inga against him and wrapped his arms around her, mainly to warm her body chilled from the cool autumn air. But what he hadn't anticipated was the sensations coursing through his body as she leaned into his chest. Inga looked up and their eyes locked on each other. He couldn't pass up the opportunity to kiss her, so he leaned down and their lips met in a deep soul-searching kiss. It felt so good, so familiar, like they'd kissed a million times before. It was an eerie thought because there was no way it could be true, they'd just met a few weeks ago, and this was their first kiss. And it was definitely a kiss to remember.

As far as kisses went, it was at the top of his list.

Erik finally pulled away ending the kiss. From the corner of his eye, he spotted Olav and Karoline looking as if they were ready to head out. "I think there are a couple of people looking for us. We should go." He released her and they followed Olav and Karoline down the vineyard row.

"I can take Olav home if you want to give Inga a ride home," Karoline suggested to Erik.

"Inga, is that okay with you?" Erik asked.

"If you don't mind, that works for me," Inga answered.

The four walked to the parking lot and Inga got into Erik's SUV. The two cars headed back to Eden Prairie.

"So, did you have a nice time at the wedding?" Inga asked.

"Yes, I'm glad you invited me." Erik smiled. "I have to look at my schedule when I get back into the office on Monday and then I'll call you to reschedule our date for next week."

"Okay."

Inga appeared deep in thought and remained silent. The music played quietly in the background of the car while Erik told her about the Master Brewing Conference he'd attended.

He parked and walked around to her side of the car to open the door, then helped her step out. At her door, they stopped while she unlocked the door.

"Thanks for coming to the wedding and giving me a ride home," Inga said turning to face him.

"My pleasure." Erik leaned toward her and gave her what he anticipated being a quick kiss, but when he realized she was kissing him back, he lingered. Finally, he ended the kiss and backed away from the door slowly. "I'll call you on Monday. Bye." He turned, barely making it back to his car, then drove home. Every part of him wanted to go back to Inga and show her how a man with Viking blood could make love to her...give her body the pleasures it desired. He'd felt it in her kiss, that she was drawn to him as much as he was drawn to her. However, this wasn't 1000 AD, he needed to wait and see how everything played out in their relationship before overstepping any of the moral boundaries of the twenty-first century.

CHAPTER 15

Inga watched Erik back out of her driveway, then walked into her townhouse and closed the door. She was beside herself. Earlier, when he'd mentioned rescheduling their date, she'd had no idea what to say to him. The kiss was in the wow category, but living in Norway? Did she want to see him again? Definitely. Did she want him to kiss her again? Absolutely.

What had just happened between them? Heck, if she knew. She'd gotten her kiss and boy... what a kiss it was! Their attraction to each other felt so intense and the passion in the kisses was incredible. She had been sorely tempted to invite him in. Visions of this strong virile man, with Viking blood coursing through his veins, making love to her, flooded her mind. She had no doubts their union would be extremely pleasurable. The weird thing was that the kiss had seemed familiar in a strange way. Her whole body wanted him and his kisses. She felt like she remembered being kissed by him many times before, but that couldn't be. They'd only just met. Maybe it was the wine getting to her? All she knew was that she didn't want to lose him.

When he'd asked her if she wanted to get married, it was as if her ears had played a trick on her. She thought he was actually asking her to marry him and every ounce of her being wanted to say *YES!* And it would be not even taking into consideration that if she married him, she'd have to say yes to living in Norway part time. What a mess! How could she live in a country where she couldn't even speak their language? Much less the fact that she'd never even been there before. People learned other languages all the time, but could she do it?

Then she thought about her great-grandmother, Gyda, who'd been born in Norway but came to America when she was just eighteen to marry a man, she'd never even met. Gyda didn't know the language, but she'd studied hard and learned English. Norwegian had always been her first language and she still had her Norwegian accent up until the day she died. It must've been extremely difficult to make the decision to leave her home back at the turn of the century. *Now we have airplanes to make travel easier and cell phones so we can call anywhere in the world at very low costs. It had to be a much easier move to make in this day and age.*

Was she trying to convince herself to move to Norway? He hadn't even actually asked her yet which meant she had plenty of time to think about, so she intended to stop thinking about it.

Inga undressed and within minutes, she was asleep in her bed.

Sunday was her only day during the week she had time to clean, do laundry and run errands. At the local Lunds & Byerlys grocery store, while buying groceries, she saw a poster for of all things a Lutefisk Dinner at Mt. Olivet Lutheran Church in Minneapolis. It was next week on Saturday from 3-7 p.m. The all-you-can-eat buffet dinner included: Lutefisk, Swedish meatballs, rutabagas, boiled potatoes, pickled beets, and Scandinavian pastries.

She'd been to a few Lutefisk dinners through the years with her parents but it had been quite a while since the last one she'd attended. The Lutefisk dinners were popular throughout Minnesota where many of the Norwegian immigrants had settled bringing their old traditions with them. She'd read a few articles in the local Minneapolis newspaper about the Lutefisk dinners not being very popular in Norway today. It sounded like this dinner might be a fun date with Erik. When he called on Monday, she would bring it up and see if he'd be interested in going.

On Friday night, Unique Events was in charge of the Edina Art Gallery's showing for October Fest consisting of local artist's renderings of local October Fest events. It was an evening showing so they would be in charge of the wine, appetizers and mini desserts. This was their first event with an art gallery so they wanted to make a good showing at the event. The gallery was expecting around 200 people to walk through during the four-hour time window from four to eight. Inga was excited that they would be serving Next Chapter Winery's wine for the event.

Monday afternoon, Erik called. "Hi, hope you got some rest after all your hard work at the wedding."

"I slept in on Sunday and tried to take it easy in the afternoon."

"I wanted to check in with you to see if we could set up a night that we could get together for dinner this week," Erik said.

"We have an event on Friday night at an art gallery in Edina. But I'd like to take you to a special dinner on Saturday night, if you're game to try something very different to most of the country, but common in Minnesota."

"Really? Sounds like you're not going to tell me what it is."

"Nope. It'll be a surprise. What do you say, are you up for it?"

"You've piqued my curiosity. I'll try almost anything once, so sure I'll go. What time should I pick you up on Saturday?"

"Does four work for you?" Inga asked.

"Sounds good. Jeans okay?"

"Yes. I'll see on Saturday afternoon."

"It's a date. See you then." Erik disconnected the call.

Inga spent the week tying up loose ends for the Art Gallery event and the Halloween, *Skol on All Hallow's Eve,* event. She even managed to get to the gym twice to work out. On Wednesday, she stopped out at Next Chapter Winery to make sure everything was on track for the wine to be delivered on Friday around noon at the art gallery.

"Sara, good to see you. Hope everything is going better for you now that the wedding is over."

"Much better. Thanks so much for taking over everything so smoothly without a hitch at the last minute. You are a life saver."

"No problem. Glad to help out. Just wanted to check that everything is set for Friday at the art gallery."

"Nellie will be bringing the wine and glasses along with the portable bar stand. She will be doing the serving. We procured the license, so we should be all set."

"Great. How is Amy doing with the baby?"

"Good. I talked to her this morning. She said she's very tired, which is to be expected with a newborn. Where are you headed next?"

"I'm on my way to Legends Country Club to go over an event they're doing for Christmas."

"Thanks for recommending us for the Art Gallery event. Let me know if you need us for any Holiday events. Winter is always our slow time, so we are open to any events you need us for serving wine."

Her meeting at Legends went well and it looked like they would be hiring Unique Events for all the golf club's event planning which would include weddings and parties. This would be big for her company. Inga and Karoline had been planning weddings for years. It was a big part of an event planner's business clientele. Many country clubs were making the move to hiring event planning companies instead of having their own on staff event planner due to the turnover in these job positions. After a few fiascos when the planners left unexpectedly, causing wedding disasters and extremely unhappy bridezillas, it was in their best interest to have a company that had multiple people on staff who knew the specifics for the weddings that had been planned.

She couldn't wait to tell Karoline the good news.

Friday came quickly and she arrived at the art gallery at noon.

Nellie arrived with the portable bar in a trailer hooked to her SUV and promptly unloaded everything. The wine bar was ready to go by two.

The catering company arrived at two with appetizers and desserts. They were set up and ready to serve by three thirty. The artist had arrived at three and was busy making sure the artwork was hung properly. He was predominantly interested in making sure the price tags were on the right paintings and easily readable.

Patrons began showing up at four and a steady stream continued until eight. They hadn't run out of food or wine, so all was good. The artist sold a fair amount of paintings for a sizeable amount so he was in a particularly good mood when they closed the doors a little after eight.

Inga was pleased and headed home about nine, shortly after Nellie and the caterer had packed, loaded their things into trailers and left. Tomorrow was Saturday and she was looking forward to sharing the evening with Erik. She hoped he liked the Lutefisk dinner she was taking him to and couldn't help looking forward, hopefully, to another kiss. She'd take his kisses any day.

CHAPTER 16

S aturday morning started out cloudy but cleared nicely by midafternoon. Inga couldn't wait to see Erik. She cleaned up her townhouse till it was spotlessly clean, just in case she invited Erik inside when he picked her up. Everything needed to be perfect because she wanted to make a good impression on him. The Lutefisk dinner wouldn't last all night so she thought maybe she could invite him in for a glass of wine when he dropped her off afterwards.

Now, she just had to decide what to wear. Decisions, decisions. He'd asked about jeans so she picked out a pair of her tapered jeans that were designed to fit like a glove and be tucked inside boots. It was cool outside so she chose a brown sweater that just happened to have a border that bore some resemblance to the Scandic designs. Her new cinnamon leather knee high leather boots would match perfectly with her new leather jacket.

Her makeup and hair finished, Inga dressed and selected a purse before going to the kitchen where she set out candles, but she didn't light them; they were for later. He would be there any minute according to the text he'd just sent her.

The doorbell rang and she opened the door. "Please come in for a minute while I grab my coat."

"Sure." He stepped inside. "You have a nice place. It has a warm feeling to it. I like it."

"Thanks." Inga walked back into her bedroom to get her jacket.

"You look really nice." Erik flashed her a big smile.

"Thanks, so do you. Are you ready for your surprise dinner?"

"Can't wait." Erik followed her out to his SUV and helped her in since it sat a bit high off the ground for her, then walked around to the driver's side and stepped up in.

"Ready?" Inga asked.

"You'll have to navigate since I have no idea where we are going."

"Just get back on the freeway, take the France Avenue exit and go north."

"Got it." Erik backed out of her driveway and headed for the freeway.

Once they were on France Avenue, Inga gave more directions, "Take a left on 50th Street."

He did and after a couple of miles, she said, "You can park in this parking lot."

"We're going to church? Is this your church?" he asked.

"Yes and no. We're going to dinner here."

They got out of the SUV and walked to the church doors where signs were posted for the Lutefisk Dinner.

"Ah. Lutefisk. I've heard of it." Erik couldn't help chuckling. "So, do you like Lutefisk?"

"I think so. I hope so. Well, let's say it's been quite a few years since I've been to one of these dinners, so we'll have to see. Mostly, I think it's the gelatin appearance of the fish that discourages many people from even tasting it. Although, I hear the meatballs are quite tasty."

They reached the doors and Erik opened them for her.

Inga walked over to the table to pick up the tickets she'd ordered and paid for online. The lady handed her an envelope containing the tickets.

They followed the line of people down the steps to the church basement where the buffet line was located. Both Inga and Erik gracefully accepted a full serving of all the offerings and found a couple of empty seats at a table.

"This all looks really good." Erik picked up his fork. "I'm trying the Lutefisk first." He'd opted for both the white sauce and melted butter sauce.

Inga left her fork on the table and watched in anticipation as he took a bite.

"Not bad," he said. "To be completely honest, I've had it in Norway. The tradition had died back home but because the American Norwegians had kept the tradition alive, restaurants started serving it during the Christmas season. Years ago, I remember my American grandmother making it, too."

Inga picked up her fork and took a bite. It didn't seem as bad as everyone had made it out to be. And obviously by the number of people at the dinner enjoying it, there were a lot of people who liked it. Maybe she'd acquired a taste for it from going to dinners back in the day with her parents and grandparents. Nowadays, her parents took off for the warmer climate of Arizona in the winter so they couldn't attend the dinners in the Minneapolis area, so she'd quit going to them.

"I think it's okay," Inga stated.

Erik laughed. "Try the meatballs, they are excellent."

They ate and joked about the Nordic traditions and how Lutefisk had become an iconic food among the Scandinavians.

The people seated across from them and next to them joined in the conversation. One of the ladies sitting directly across the table had actually written a book about Lutefisk named, *Real Norwegians Eat Lutefisk*, and gave Inga her business card. It would be fun to go online and check out the book.

For dessert, there was another table filled with Scandinavian pastries. Various assortments of lefse, krumkake, sandbakels, Kringla, fattigmann, rommegrot, and rosettes beckoned to them. They took one of each to sample.

"Do you know how to make any of these?" Erik asked.

"My mother taught me how to make Krumkake. She used to make

a few of the others but I've never tried making them. Are you familiar with all of them?"

"Oh, yah. They are common in Norway. My mother makes all of them plus a few others like the heart shaped waffles. They are my favorite and quite popular back home."

"My mother makes the almond cake using my grandmother's recipe. I was thinking I should ask her for the recipe and trying making it."

"If you travel to Norway. . .with me, I'm sure my mother would go on a baking spree for us."

"That sounds fun and delicious."

After finishing all their pastries, they left feeling stuffed.

When Erik pulled into her driveway, she got up her courage to ask him to come in. "It's still early, if you'd like to come in for a glass of wine from our favorite winery, Next Chapter, you're welcome to."

"Sure, I think I might have to start liking wine. But never more than ale." He gave her a wink as he parked and they walked into her townhouse.

"Have a seat and I'll pour our wine."

Erik sat down on the couch and picked up a photo album neatly placed on the coffee table. "Okay if look at your photos?" He motioned to the photo book in his hand.

"Sure, they're photos of the events Karoline and I have done through the years. I always take a couple photos for the book at each one." Inga set out coasters on the coffee table, then set the filled wine glasses on them and sat down next to Erik.

"It appears you and Karoline have done quite a few events. You must enjoy your work."

"It doesn't even feel like a job when you are doing something you love."

Erik continued looking at the pictures while Inga explained the themes of each one and where they were located. Before they knew it, it was ten.

"I should probably get going," Erik said. "Thanks for treating me to a Lutefisk dinner. I had a great time." He got up and walked to the door while Inga followed him.

"My pleasure."

She was standing directly in front of him near the door when he leaned down and kissed her, pulling her gently against his chest.

Inga wrapped her arms around his back while the kiss deepened. Every inch of her body wanted to guide him to the bedroom, but of course it was too soon and it wasn't the proper thing to do. She decided to just enjoy the moment and kissed him back with all the passion bottled up inside her for the past years.

"I should probably get going," he repeated as he ended the kiss and released her.

Inga stepped back reluctantly agreeing with him.

"I have to be in Colorado next week for some meetings and won't get back until Sunday. Would it be okay though, if I call you and we can talk?" he asked.

"Certainly." Inga smiled as he left and closed the door.

Inga was in love. She already knew this. She was done looking. Erik was the one she'd been looking for her whole life. Now she just needed to find out how he felt. And maybe she should see if there were some online Norwegian language courses she could take. The real question that needed to be answered... was could she leave her home in America?

CHAPTER 17

Early Monday morning Inga and Karoline arrived at the office to go over the *Skol on All Hallow's Eve* event to make sure everything was taken care of because if anything wasn't handled, it needed to be dealt with promptly. Then, they needed to move on to the event for Saturday at the Lafayette Club on Lake Minnetonka.

It was a 50th Anniversary party, being put on by the couple's two daughters. These types of events tended to be the easier ones, especially if the families came from money and their parties included a sit-down dinner with a full bar and appetizers. The cake on order from Specialty Cakes resembled a multi-tiered wedding cake. Later, a live band would perform for the guests to showcase their ballroom dancing expertise.

"So how did the *Lutefisk Dinner* date go?" Karoline asked.

"Really well." Inga smiled brightly.

"I hear *Lutefisk* tastes pretty bad. Did you eat it?"

"I think it's an acquired taste. I've eaten it when I was younger, so to me it tasted okay. Don't get me wrong, I'd never say it's the best food in the world. Erik's eaten it before, too."

"Well, I guess that's good. So, you had a good time?"

"Oh, it was a great night all around."

"More kisses?" Karoline probed.

"Definitely. Like I said before, he's a really good kisser." Excitement radiated from her body.

"Maybe Olav and I should try one of these dinners?"

"You said you were interested in some of the Norwegian foods and this would be a great place to taste a variety of them."

"I'll have to mention it to Olav and check online for some upcoming Lutefisk dinner locations out this way." Karoline's phone rang so she walked out and down the hall to her office to take the call.

On Thursday, Inga's package arrived containing the Viking costume she'd ordered from an Etsy online shop. She'd received the email confirming it was delivered and couldn't wait to get home to try it on. At four, she left the office and stopped at DSW shoes to look for a pair of boots to go with it. After trying on several pairs, she chose a comfortable black pair with a vintage design look to them. She spotted the package on her doorstep as she pulled into the garage. Quickly exiting the car, she picked up the package and immediately tore it open once inside her kitchen.

The dress and apron looked exactly like the pictures online and were just what she'd anticipated. She walked directly into her bedroom carrying the costume and quickly changed into it. The costume fit perfectly, except it needed a belt. She picked one from her belt rack and put it on. Next, she put the boots on and stepped in front of the mirror. The woman staring back at her looked like a Viking woman from 1000 A.D. It could be totally possible that she resembled one of her female ancestors. After all, they would have some of the same DNA and since her grandmother came from Norway, she would have Viking DNA. She'd never considered doing one of the Ancestry DNA tests, but now she thought it would be definitely something she should do just for fun.

On Saturday, she met Karoline at the Lafayette around noon. The party started at two, but there wasn't much to do. The country club had its own bar and kitchen staff for the food. They were pretty much there just to make sure everything happened as planned and if there were any issues, the staff would take care of them.

The Walbergs arrived at one-thirty and greeted them cordially and aristocratically. It was almost like they came from royalty, but they seemed to be a very sweet couple who'd probably been through it all and had stayed together regardless. Whether it was for love or just what was expected of them, they'd made it for fifty years and were still smiling which said a lot.

Erik had called on Wednesday night and they'd talked for almost an hour. He filled her in on his business meetings with the beer wholesalers in Denver. It sounded like he'd made good progress in persuading them to give his company, Nordic Brewing, an opportunity to sell the Nordic brew products at the liquor stores in Colorado. She hadn't heard from him since that call, but hoped he'd call her later that night.

The anniversary party went well with no problems. There was more than enough food so the staff along with her and Karoline were treated to steak dinners rather than discarding the leftovers.

Inga was home by seven where she promptly kicked off her shoes and changed into PJs. She'd brought home a piece of the decadent multi-layered chocolate cake, sat down on the couch with a glass of milk and clicked on the TV to the Hallmark Channel. She was in the mood for a good romance movie.

Around eight, the phone rang. She looked at the caller ID and saw it was Erik. She pressed the button to pause the movie and tapped the phone to take the call. "Hello."

"How are you? How was your event?"

"It went very well. They were a sweet couple celebrating their 50th wedding anniversary."

"That's a long time."

"I know. It's hard to imagine fifty years when you're only thirty."

"I thought ladies never tell their age?"

"I'm not ashamed of my age, why wouldn't I tell?"

"Since we're talking ages, I suppose I should tell you mine."

"Only if you want to."

"I'm thirty-five. Anything else you'd like to know?"

"Nope, I'm good. How'd the rest of your meetings go?"

"The trip was very successful, Viking Blonde Ale along with our other ales will be offered in Colorado starting next month."

"Congratulations. I'm happy for you."

"Well, I have an early flight tomorrow so I need to get some sleep, but I just wanted to see how your event went. I'll call you next week."

"Okay, talk to you next week." Inga tapped the phone to end the call. Dang, but she really liked Erik and she couldn't wait to see him. Probably wouldn't be until next Saturday for the *Skol on All Hallow's Eve* event at the apple orchard. She really hoped he liked her new Viking costume.

Inga clicked the movie back on and snuggled under her blanket to watch the rest of her fall romance movie. She managed to stay awake to see the movie's happy ending, then went straight to bed hoping her and Erik would get a happy ending, too.

CHAPTER 18

Monday morning Inga and Karoline were busy going over everything for the *Skol on All Hallow's Eve* event. Inga felt like this one was her *baby*. She'd poured her heart and soul into it, bringing to it the love she had for her family's Norwegian heritage, predominantly the food. And particularly her Viking costume, of course, which was a big part of the event for her. She opened the Jensrud Apple Orchard folder on her desk first with the paper copies, for everything pertaining to the event, then powered up her laptop.

One by one, she went over the vendor contractors they were using and sent out confirmation emails. Replies popped in almost immediately from them stating everything was on track and they would see her on Saturday at ten. They all needed to be there then and be ready to go by eleven.

It looked like it would be a long day, but hopefully lots of fun. She sent off her last email to Erik confirming his brew tent for the event.

He informed her that he wasn't going to be working the tent but would be there to oversee it and was looking forward to seeing her.

She could hardly wait to see him and show off her new Viking costume.

Midafternoon on Wednesday, she had a meeting with Darla at the Jensrud Apple Orchard. When she arrived at one, the parking lot was full. It was a beautiful sunny fall day with temps in the low seventies. According to the weather forecast the clear skies and warm temps were supposed to hold out until Sunday. So, it looked good for the Saturday event. Well, if weather forecasts could be believed and actually came true. Regardless, she was hoping for the best.

Inga walked into the apple barn now filled with different varieties of apples and of course pumpkins for Halloween. "Darla, good to see you. How is everything going for Saturday?"

"Good. We'll start setting up on Friday, so we should have everything in place by the time you and your vendors arrive on Saturday morning."

"I just saw the weather forecast and it looks good for Saturday."

"Me, too. I'm so hoping for at least no rain. Rain kind of puts a damper on everything."

"I agree. I see the advertising signs and flags are set out. They look good. Have you been getting any interest in the event from your customers?"

"Oh, yes. Many have said they will be coming back on Saturday. A lot of them seem to like the Viking theme. The Vikings seem to be quite popular lately. I think we'll have a pretty good turnout."

"Sounds like you have everything under control on your part. Let me know if anything comes up on Friday when you're setting up."

"I will. Better get back to work. It looks like they have a long line at the register. I'll call you Friday if I have any questions or need anything. Grab a few apples to take with you on your way out."

"Bye, see you Saturday. Oh, and thanks for the apples." Inga slowly meandered through the barn picking up a couple of the Honey Crisp apples, which were her favorite.

Once in her car, she wiped the apple with a napkin and took a bite, savoring the cool crisp apple flavor before heading home.

Before they knew it, Friday was upon them. Inga and Karoline went over everything for the *Skol on All Hallow's Eve* event one more time. They checked in once more via text and email with all the vendors. So far, so good. Everyone had replied and there were no issues, for now.

"What are you wearing to the event?" Inga asked.

"I've been trying to decide. I have a costume I got a few years back at the Renaissance Fair. It's not Viking but it is from the medieval time period, so I think it should work."

"Did I tell you I ordered a Viking costume?"

"Really? Is it one of those sexy Valkyrie ones I've seen online?" Karoline asked.

"No. I decided to go with the style the actual Viking women wore during the Viking Age. I ordered it and I think it looks pretty authentic. I didn't find a cloak though, so I hope I won't be freezing."

"Sounds interesting. I know you mentioned ordering one, but wasn't sure what you decided on. Can't wait to see it. But are you going to wear it all day?"

"That's what I'm trying to decide. What do you think we should do?" Inga asked.

"I'm thinking I'd rather wear jeans while we are running around helping set up and bring the costume along to change into later."

"I like that idea. Let's do that. I'm excited for Erik to see it," Inga said.

"I'm sure he'll like anything you wear. According to Olav, he's pretty intrigued by you. So, if you can figure out this whole thing about living in Norway part time, I think Erik may be the guy for you."

"I really like him. I'm even thinking about taking Norwegian language classes."

"Wow! I'm excited for you. Hope this works out for both of you."

CHAPTER 19

Inga had trouble falling asleep since she couldn't stop going over everything in her head for the *Skol on All Hallow's Eve* event. The whole event had fallen into place so easily, she was scared she might've forgotten something important. Finally, her body gave in and she fell asleep.

At seven, she woke up and began preparing for the big day.

She put on a pair of jeans and knee-high boots. Then selected a brown, rust and orange plaid flannel shirt. For a jacket, she set out her Unique Events windproof lined jacket complete with their logo. Hey, free advertising was free advertising and nothing to balk at.

After having a bagel and coffee, she checked her emails and texts. Nothing yet, so hopefully everything was still good. She sent Karoline a text saying she'd meet her at the orchard at nine and got a text back instantaneously with a confirmation that she'd be there.

Inga took the garment bag containing the Viking costume out of her closet and set it on the back of the breakfast bar stool then grabbed the bag with her boots she'd bought to wear with it. Trying to think if there was anything else she might need, she returned to her closet and selected a small black leather purse with a long strap.

Karoline and Inga arrived about the same time.

The two food trucks were already there and setting up in their assigned places. A pickup truck with a trailer from Nordic Brewing pulled in a few minutes later. Mark, the business manager at Nordic Brewing, got out and began setting up.

Inga walked over to greet him, "Hi. I'm Inga. Let me know if you have any questions or need anything."

Mark grinned at her. "We met at Valhalla Nordic Smoke and Ale House."

"Oh yes, I remember now."

"Erik wanted me to let you know he won't be here until eleven."

"Thanks. I'll let you get set up." She walked back toward the building.

Another pickup and trailer pulled in, apparently with the band as their name, *Skandik Blues*, was printed in large letters on the side of the trailer. Immediately, Karoline approached the pickup and directed them where to park and unload, as they would be in the barn.

Inga and Karoline supervised the set up to make sure everything went as they had planned.

People were starting to arrive already since the apple orchard opened at ten. But by then, all her vendors were set up and ready to go. She glanced down toward the barn and truly liked what she saw. It was just as she'd envisioned. She'd ordered feather flags for each vendor stating their name and what they were selling. The flags were a rust color with gold print. So, she'd ordered one for each vendor: Nordic Treats / Lapskaus, The Onion Blossom / Onion Hay Stacks, Jensrud Apple Orchard / Mini Fried Apple Pies, Skandik Blues Band and Nordic Brewing / Viking Blonde Ale. Yes, she'd out done herself with this one. They looked professional and extremely inviting.

"Looks great," Erik said as he walked up beside her. "Good job!"

"Thanks. I put a lot of love and effort into this. I consider it my Viking baby." Inga chuckled.

"Looks like it's going to be perfect weather and there is already a large crowd."

"I see you have your Viking costume on already. I should go and change into mine."

"Oh, you found one you liked?"

"Yes. I hope you like it. I went with the more authentic style. I'll catch up with you later."

"I'm going to check with Mark and see if he needs anything."

"Oh, and by the way, you look great in that costume. Did anyone ever tell you that you look like Thor?"

Erik burst out laughing. "A few times." He smiled at her and walked away.

Inga went to her car to get the Viking costume, then found an employee restroom where she could change. When she opened the door, she saw Karoline had beaten her there and was already in her medieval costume. "That looks great on you, Karoline."

"Thanks, hurry and change so I can see yours," Karoline said as she continued fixing her hair.

Inga stepped into the bathroom stall and changed. She brought her boots out in her hand. "What do you think?"

"I love it. Very authentic looking. It fits you perfect. You have a way of making anything you wear look sexy even when it isn't."

"Thanks, I think." Inga laughed.

"Erik's going to love it. I saw him a bit ago and he had his costume on. He definitely looks like Thor in his costume."

"Didn't I tell you he did?"

"Yes, but sometimes you just have to see it for yourself."

"Is Olav here yet?" Inga asked.

"No, he won't get here until two. I think he might be doing some last-minute costume shopping. We'll see when he gets here, just what he came up with."

Inga finished putting her boots on and changed her purse to the smaller one she'd brought along. "I'm going to put this stuff back in my car. Are you ready?"

"Yes."

Inga and Karoline walked back to their cars in the parking lot to drop off their clothes.

The parking lot was full and people had begun parking along the road and on the grass. They walked back to where the vendors were busy serving customers who were lined up to get the delicious food the vendors were serving. Each vendor had posted pictures of the food they were offering and it looked delicious.

Inga had been waiting to taste them but decided to come back later when there was a smaller line or no line at all. Right now, was lunch time so it was busy.

Inga and Karoline stopped in the barn to listen to Skandik Blues playing their mellow music to a larger than expected crowd. To her surprise, the band members had donned Viking style garb to go with her Viking Halloween costume theme. At the end of the song, she clapped and gave them the thumbs up sign. She watched them nod in acknowledgement.

Behind the barn was the bonfire ready to be lit at five when the sun would begin setting and the temps would most likely drop to the fifties. They stopped to check it out and determined it was ready to go.

The crowds were much larger than any of them anticipated, probably due to the good weather they'd been blessed with. She'd spotted Erik in the Nordic Brewing tent that was set up in front of their trailer. He was busy serving ale since Mark was swamped. He nodded as they passed by.

It was almost four when they finally were able to sample the Lapskaus and Onion Hay Stacks. They both were delicious. Thankfully, the vendors had come prepared for a large crowd and still had plenty of food left to sell.

Around six, new customers were arriving. These were more adults and less children. Many had Viking costumes and appeared to be having a great time.

Sadly, Erik had ended up helping Mark most of the day so she hadn't had a chance to talk to him. The event ended at nine and it was almost eight when she made it back to the bonfire. The temps had been steadily dropping and she was sorely wishing she'd found a cloak to buy to go with her costume. She walked over closer to the bonfire to get warm and began rubbing her hands together near the fire.

She heard someone come up behind her and turned to see Erik. He had something in his hands but she couldn't make out what it was exactly.

"I heard through the grapevine you didn't have a cloak to go with your costume and I thought you might need one."

"Is this yours?"

"Yes, but I have two. I brought and extra one back from Norway, the last time I was there. I have no idea why, but for some reason I thought I might need it." He gently placed the cloak over her shoulders.

"I don't know what to say. Thank you. I am a bit chilled as you can see." She pulled it closed in front and looked for a hood of some kind, but didn't find one.

"Here let me help you. They are meant to be fastened with a brooch like this." He held it out to show her. "They're kind of tricky to work, let me do it for you."

Inga moved in front of him and away from the fire a bit. She held the cloak in place for him. Erik stuck the pin through both layers and latched it together. As soon as he latched it onto the cloak, eerie sensations passed through both of their bodies simultaneously since his hands were still on the brooch.

Visions of Erik and Inga dressed in Viking clothes standing at the front of a Viking ship, holding hands flashed through their minds. They kissed and it was evident they were man and wife.

Erik looked into Inga's eyes, searching to see if she'd somehow experienced the vision also. Her eyes were searching his for answers at the same time. He took her in his arms and kissed her just as they'd done in the vision. They kissed for a long time, while they were lost in a vortex of sensations and memories.

Finally, in the distance, he heard Olav give a fake cough. He ended the kiss, stepped back, and turned to face Olav.

"Mark sent me to find you. He could really use some help serving ale."

Erik looked back at Inga with pure longing in his eyes.

"I can help instead if you'd like," Olav offered.

"I'll go." He turned back towards Inga. "We need to talk. I'll find you later." Erik reluctantly walked away.

Inga stood watching him. What had just happened? She had to be going crazy. She'd just seen herself on a Viking ship with Erik and it appeared to be in the past. Like over a thousand years ago. That couldn't be! What was happening? He'd kissed her just like they'd done on the ship. Hell, she hadn't even drunk any ale yet, so it wasn't that.

Someone from your past will reappear in your life. Your true soul mate. With him, you will experience a love that surpasses time.

"Everything okay?" Olav asked turning to look at her.

"I'm not sure."

"What does that mean?"

"I don't know." Her hand reached up to the brooch wondering if it had anything to do with it. "I'm fine." She turned away and went in search of Karoline.

She found Karoline inside where it was much warmer.

"I need to talk to you." Inga took Karoline's hand and practically pulled her into one of the empty offices.

"Okay." Karoline followed her. "What's going on?"

"I'm losing my mind, Karoline."

"Did something happen?"

"I was by the bonfire and Erik gave me a cloak to wear because I was cold."

"I told him you didn't have one, so he must've got it for you."

"I'm not sure about that, but when he used his brooch, that looked like it came from the Viking Era, to fasten the cloak so it stayed in place, I saw a vision of him and I standing on a Viking ship kissing."

"Don't know what to say. Are you sure?"

"Yes, and it appeared that we were husband and wife. Karoline, the people I saw on the ship looked identical to me and Erik. What can that mean?"

"I have no idea."

"In September at the James J. Hill Days, on a lark, I went into a gypsy fortune teller's trailer...the fortune she gave me was very strange."

"What? You didn't tell me."

"It seemed really stupid and everyone knows they don't come true. But the strange thing is that when her hand touched mine, I felt the same strange sensations that happened when I first met Erik. And come to think of it, they happen whenever we touch and then fade. When he touched me to put the brooch on the sensations were intense and even more so when he kissed me."

"What was the fortune, Inga?"

"Someone from your past will reappear in your life. Your true soul mate. With him, you will experience a love that surpasses time."

"Do you believe in magic?" Karoline asked.

"I didn't. But now, I'm not so sure."

"It could be your fortune's coming true. Maybe sometime in your past, you and Erik were married and soul mates, which would be a love that surpasses time when you find each other again. Who knows maybe the Viking DNA passed down through the years has now produced the same people as back then and somehow, you've found each other again."

"The scary part is that is actually making sense somewhat. So, I must be crazy," Inga concluded.

"I don't think you're crazy. Do you think he saw the same vision?" Karoline asked.

"He didn't say anything. Olav came and said Mark needed him, so he left and said we needed to talk later."

"It sounds like he might have. So, let's go back out there and finish up our jobs. You can talk to Erik later and maybe the two of you can figure out what happened by the bonfire. Alright?" Karoline asked.

"Sure."

Inga and Karoline put on their game faces and went out to finish their event up properly. Things were winding down and it was almost nine.

The vendors closed up quickly at nine and left. It had been a long and busy day and she was sure everyone was plenty tired. She certainly was. The Nordic Brewing trailer appeared to be loaded and ready to go.

Inga watched as Mark pulled out of the parking lot with the trailer. Now, she just needed to find Erik. She looked toward the barn and spotted him through the doors where the fire was still burning. The full moon provided a lot of light when you were out of town even a few miles. He turned and saw her. She walked towards the fire where he waited for her.

"Hi. I think we need to have a long in-depth conversation about what happened." Erik took her hand in his.

"Yes, we do," Inga acknowledged.

"But not now. It's late and I think we're both tired. We have a lot to think about and discuss."

"I agree." Fear radiated through her body. She was scared but could think of no reason why.

"How about I pick you up for dinner tomorrow night and we'll talk?"

"There's a restaurant by my house called Wildfire. They have nice private booths. We should be able to get one on a Sunday night."

"That will work. I'll pick you up at six." He pulled her into his arms and kissed her.

She felt like she was melting in his arms.

He gently released her. "See you tomorrow." He walked away.

Karoline and Olav watched from a distance, waiting to see what would happen. After Erik walked away, Olav waited as Karoline walked over to Inga.

"Everything okay?" Karoline asked.

"Yes. We're going to dinner tomorrow night to discuss what happened."

"Well, that's good because that means something happened for him, too."

"Hadn't thought of that," Inga stated.

"The kiss looked good and I know how much you like a good kisser."

"Yes, it was good."

Inga, Karoline, and Olav walked to their cars in the parking lot without saying a word, and left.

CHAPTER 20

Inga could barely contain the emotions raging through her body. Her life had just been turned upside down. By a kiss? By a brooch from the past?

She pulled into her driveway and opened the garage door. Strangely, she didn't even remember driving home. Weird how your body can go into auto pilot when it needs to and it definitely had gotten her home safe and sound. Once inside her townhouse, she walked straight into the bedroom to undress. Standing in front of her mirror, she stared at the woman's image reflecting back at her. Had it really been her? Or the better question to ask was what if she was really someone else from another time?

The Viking dress fell to the floor but she left it there and put her PJs on. Not even taking time to wash her make up off, she crawled into bed and turned the light off. Her body was spent and she just couldn't think about what happened at the bonfire anymore tonight. Tomorrow, she would try to figure it out and, hopefully, Erik had some answers for her. Within minutes she was fast asleep.

The morning sun was peeking in behind her curtains when she finally woke up at nine. Her body knew it needed to rest which is why she'd probably slept so soundly. A hot shower sounded wonderful so she headed for the bathroom.

An hour later, she was seated at her breakfast bar with an English muffin and a cup of coffee staring blankly at the TV. Nothing had changed. The world was just as crazy as before, only now she was crazy, too.

Her phone rang around noon. She glanced over to see who was calling and saw Karoline's name. She swiped at her phone. "Hello."

"So how is Inga, this bright sunny morning?"

"Awake, but that's all I can say for now."

"Good. Did you sleep?" Karoline asked.

"Yes, like I was dead to the world. Oh, that sounds bad, doesn't it? You know what I mean."

"Any thoughts about last night?"

"Nope. Just that I'm probably crazy and losing my mind."

"Probably, you're not either."

"But, really would you be able to even tell?"

"Why don't you take it easy, watch a little TV and before you know it, it'll be time for Erik to pick you up?" Karoline suggested.

"That sounds good."

"If you need me for anything, just call. If not, I'll see you at the office tomorrow."

"Ok, bye." Inga disconnected the call and moved to the couch to watch a Hallmark movie. At least they made sense and she knew the ending would be happy. There wasn't much else she could be sure of at this point, but she could always count on Hallmark.

Inga made it through two movies, then it was time to get out of her robe and put some clothes on before Erik arrived.

She needed to shake her negative mood caused by the vision she'd seen of her and Erik on a Viking ship while standing in front of the bonfire. At least, she hoped that was the reason. Being deemed a crazy lady, who saw visions, wasn't on her list of desired attributes. To say the least, she was a bit freaked out by the whole thing. Was the vision even real? Erik was real and he was the one for her. She knew that now and desperately hoped he could help her understand what had happened last night when he fastened the cloak closed with his brooch at the bonfire. She instantly prayed she wasn't going crazy. But more than anything she hoped he'd seen the vision, too.

The doorbell rang at six.

Excited and a bit nervous, she walked to the door with her leather jacket and purse in her hand.

"Hi, how was your day?" he asked as she locked the door behind her.

"As well as could be expected after the crazy night we had."

"Let's wait until we get to the restaurant to discuss last night." Erik opened her door and helped her into his SUV.

Apparently, Erik had called to make a reservation, so they were promptly seated in one of the private booths after they arrived.

The waiter brought water and a bottle of wine which he poured into their wine glasses. "I'll be back to take your order," he said and left.

Inga and Erik sat staring at each other. Neither speaking.

Finally, Inga picked up her menu to find something to order. She hadn't eaten since breakfast and that was just an English muffin. Out of the corner of her eye, she saw Erik pick up his menu.

Then the waiter returned and took their orders.

Erik took a sip of his wine. "We should talk about last night."

"Where would you like to start?"

"Let's start with this. Whenever we touch, I feel strange sensations pulse through my body."

Inga smiled, finally. "Me, too. I'm glad it's not just me. I thought I was ill or going crazy."

"From the first day we met, I felt drawn to you. Don't take this wrong, but I felt like you were mine. Like I wanted you and there was some special bond between us. I thought I was crazy, too."

Inga stared into his eyes. "When you kissed me the first time, it felt familiar, like we'd kissed a thousand times before, but we'd just met. So, I knew that wasn't possible."

He nodded. "Each time we kissed, I was so drawn to you. I wanted to make love to you so badly. It seemed like it would have been appropriate in the Viking Era but not in our century. I had to use every ounce of self-control I had to walk away." Erik smiled at her.

"I wanted you to make love to me, too. But I knew it was too soon. We barely knew each other."

"Last night by the fire, when I pinned the brooch on the cloak, my desire for you increased tenfold. The sensations pulsing through my body were so intense, I thought I was going to have a heart attack."

"Anything else?" Inga smiled.

"Trust me, this may sound really whacky, but I saw an image of you and I standing on a Viking ship which had to be over a thousand years ago. We were dressed as the Vikings dressed back then and we were kissing. I had an uncontrollable urge to kiss you. That's when I kissed you."

"No, I don't think you're crazy because I saw the same thing. It was like a vision, almost like a movie playing in my head."

"What's going on with us? Maybe we've both lost our minds." Erik sat back in his seat and ran his fingers through his hair.

"Hopefully not," she said.

"Well, I'm not sure, yet. The brooch I pinned on the cloak you were wearing, I found it buried in the ground on my land in Norway. I was building my new house and we were digging the foundation when I saw something in the dirt reflecting the sunlight. I dug deeper to see what it was and I found the brooch. It very likely is from the Viking Era. My family has owned that piece of land for many generations."

"There has been a lot of publicity lately about DNA and ancestry. Do you think years ago there were two people who looked like us that were married and loved each other in the Viking Era?" Inga asked finally, smiling at Erik.

"That's a real possibility. Maybe my finding the brooch led me to finding you and just maybe we are really just two old souls trying to find our way back to each other?"

"Do you want to hear something even more eerie than all this?" Inga asked.

"Okay."

"Remember when we were at the James J. Hill Days event in Wayzata?" she questioned.

"Yes."

"Right before I stopped at your tent, we'd gone in the gypsy fortune teller's wagon that was at the end of the street to get our fortunes told by the gypsy."

"I remember it."

"This is what my fortune read: 'Someone from your past will reappear in your life. Your true soul mate. With him, you will experience a love that surpasses time.' And when she handed it to me, I felt like I'd been zapped by something."

"Now this is going to sound even crazier. Earlier in the day, on a lark, I went to that same fortune teller's wagon and she gave me exactly the same fortune. I, also, felt like she zapped me with an electrical current when she handed it to me."

The waiter brought their salads and bread.

If it weren't for the fact she was starving, Inga would've waited, but she absently picked up a roll and buttered it. "Do you believe in magic?" she asked and took a bite of her roll.

"No, but now, I'm questioning that belief." Erik poured dressing on his salad and took a bite.

"Right after I left her wagon, I walked down the street and stopped to get a beer at your tent. When you handed me the glass of ale and our hands touched, I felt a strange sensation flow through me."

"I did, too. But I thought it was nothing."

Their entrees came, so they changed the subject to food while they ate.

After they finished their meals, they continued their previous conversation.

"So, what conclusion have we come to?" Inga asked.

"Well, sounds like we're both most likely crazy. Our chemistry is off the charts. We were probably lovers and bonded as man and wife over a thousand years ago. Our fortunes foretold we'd be together again. And we're probably soul mates."

"Nicely put. So, where do we go from here?"

"Well, we could get married and live happily ever after." Erik flashed Inga his sexiest Thor smile.

"In America, they make movies about that and the women love them. Including me. They're called Hallmark movies and they always have a happy ending."

"So, will you marry me?" Erik asked.

"That sounds even crazier. We've only known each other for less than two months."

"Don't let that stop you when forces beyond our control are pushing us together."

"Do I have to move to Norway?" Inga asked.

"I do have a beautiful house overlooking a fjord on the Western coast of Norway. Maybe it would be beneficial for you to come and at least visit Norway first. After all, it is the home of your ancestors and mine."

"But my home is here now. I've lived in America my whole life."

"I know it would be hard for you to move, especially since you've never been there. You would need to experience Norway for yourself firsthand, before you could make a decision."

"I don't know the language, either."

"These days, everyone speaks English except the older generation, like my grandparents age, so that wouldn't be a problem. But you might like to take some classes and try to learn a little Norsk."

"I've been searching desperately for someone to love, who I could spend the rest of my life with. A man who would feel the same way about me. It seems you are that man and we are destined to be together. It would be useless to fight fate, so I'm not going to. Like you said, the chemistry between us is off the charts." She paused for a moment. "Just letting you know up front though, I'd only agree to part time in each country." Inga smiled seductively at Erik. "In this day and age that seems totally doable. So, I'm hoping you agree with this plan. If you do, I will be by your side always. Which, in our case, may mean thousands of years. Are you up for the challenge?"

"That's only fair. I can work with that. I want you to know that I fell in love with you the moment I saw you walk up to my Nordic

Brewing tent to buy a beer. It was love at first sight. Every time I saw you after that, I fell harder and when I kissed you, I was a goner. There was no looking back for me. I could only hope you would feel the same way, too."

"After the day we met, I told Karoline you were *the one* for me. I kept hoping you'd feel the same, too."

Inga and Erik left the restaurant feeling much better than they had when they'd arrived. When they arrived at Inga's townhouse, she invited him to come in.

Once inside, after the door closed behind them, they fell into each other's arms and kissed, finally making their way over to the couch. For Inga, being in Erik's arms felt so natural, like that was where she was meant to be.

"I think we need to plan a trip to Norway soon." Erik nuzzled her ear.

"Yes," Inga responded in between Erik's kisses.

"And then a wedding."

"Yes," Inga answered feeling like this was the best day of her life so far, but knowing that with Erik by her side, there would be many more to come in their future.

EPILOGUE

The following May, Inga and Erik boarded a plane to Bergen, Norway. They'd spent the past six months getting to know each other better and enjoying each other's company spending every minute they had available together. Erik wanted Inga to see Norway in the spring when it would be warm and the spectacular natural waterfalls would be flowing with full force from the pristine white snow melting off the majestic Norwegian mountains.

Erik made all the travel arrangements for their trip. His parents and grandparents were excited to meet Inga and promised to show her all the customs and traditions Norway had to offer. His mother especially was waiting to welcome another American into the family. He'd mentioned to his parents that there was something he needed to talk to them about when they were in Norway. Knowing his mother, it was probably going to drive her crazy with anticipation, but trying to explain what had happened between him and Inga with the old Viking style brooch was definitely not something you discussed over the phone.

They arrived in Bergen on May 15 and spent the night at a hotel with a view of the waterfront, so they could sleep off some of the jet lag. Erik also wanted Inga to see the highlights of the city where he'd spent considerable amounts of time, since he had cousins who lived in the area. He wanted to be sure she saw the best view of the city from Mount Fløyen, by taking the Fløibanen, a railway train that ran from the center of Bergen to the summit of the mountain and was built in 1918. For dinner, they went to the Bryggen, a waterfront dock area filled with commercial buildings and where some of the best restaurants could be found. The Bryggen was on UNESCO's World Heritage list and was one of Norway's main attractions. But the most interesting part for them would be that Bergen and its original Bryggen were founded in 1070 A.D. when the Vikings still roamed the seas. The Vikings who were their ancestors. No wonder he'd always felt at home in this city.

Erik planned for them to stay in Bergen for May 17 or Syttende Mai, Norway's Independence Day celebration. He knew the main streets would be flooded with both young and old wearing their bunads, which were colorful hand embroidered folk costumes from the various areas of Norway. There would be a parade and a smorgasbord of Norwegian foods would be sold by vendors and restaurants. This was something he wanted her to see.

Three days after landing in Norway, they arrived in Ulsteinvik by ferry and then rented a car to drive to Erik's house which faced a fjord on the Western coast of Norway. Inga had mentioned that she hoped the little bit of Norsk she'd learned would suffice, but he'd reassured her again that most of them spoke pretty good English. In the morning, she would be meeting his parents and family, but for now it was just them.

Inga stepped out of the car and was in awe. "Erik, this is so absolutely incredibly beautiful. Pictures don't do it justice."

"I knew you'd like it." He took her hand and led her down the hill to the shores of their fjord on the North Sea.

As she slowly strolled down the hill, Inga experienced an eerie feeling she'd walked on this ground before. She still wasn't sure she believed in fortune tellers or magic, but this place felt like it was where she was supposed to be. It became extremely obvious as her senses reeled with the knowledge that her ancestors existed on this very same land and bordering sea where she now stood, over a thousand years ago. A part of her could feel them surrounding her and welcoming her home. Shivers flooded her body. She looked ahead at Erik now walking in front of her and knew she was his and he was hers forever.

"What do you think?" he asked stopping and turning toward her.

"I think we should get married. I love you." She put her hand in his extended hand and moved closer to him.

"I love you and will love you for all time." Erik smiled.

"We need two weddings. One here in Norway and one in Minnesota," Inga stated gazing out at the sun hovering slightly over the horizon.

"You got it. Let's have one while we're here and one when we get back to Minnesota."

"I love you, Erik, now and forever," Inga promised.

"I love you, Inga, now and forever." He took her in his arms and they kissed while the sun cast a reddish hue in the sky that danced across the shimmering sea. The beauty of the picturesque Norwegian fjord lay serenely in front of them and the majestic mountains rested quietly behind Erik and Inga, embracing them for all eternity.

As if it was an echo from both the mountains and the sea, they heard a voice say,

"Someone from your past will reappear in your life.
Your true soul mate.
With him, you will experience a love that surpasses time."
The End

SCANDINAVIAN ALMOND CAKE

INGA'S GRANDMOTHER'S RECIPE

Ingredients
- 1 ¼ Cups sugar
- 1 egg
- 1 ½ tsp almond extract
- 2/3 Cup milk
- 1 ¼ Cups all-purpose flour
- ½ tsp baking powder
- 1 stick melted butter

Instructions

Beat sugar, egg, almond extract and milk together well. Then add flour and baking powder, blend together, add melted butter and stir.

Spray Scandinavian almond cake pan generously with non-stick baking spray. Pour batter into pan. Bake at 350 for 40-50 minutes or until edges are golden brown and toothpick inserted comes out clean. Cool for 30 minutes.

Invert onto almond cake plate and sprinkle with powdered sugar or slice, then top with whipped crème and Lingonberry sauce.

SCANDINAVIAN ALMOND CAKE

AUTHOR'S NOTE

My Norwegian heritage is a large part of my everyday life which includes my membership in the Sons of Norway, Daughters of Norway, Lakselaget, and the Norway House in Minneapolis. My father was born in Norway and after enduring his teenage years under the Nazi Occupation of Norway during WWII, he came to the United States a year after the war ended. In Minnesota we are blessed to have an abundance of Norwegian events to attend and I wanted to share a few of them with my readers. The *Scandinavian Almond Cake* is so delicious and a part of my yearly celebrations. I'm a huge connoisseur of anything that has to do with the Vikings and so proud to have the Vikings as our Minnesota NFL Football team! Finally, I found a way to include them in one of my romance stories. I hope you enjoy Inga and Erik's Viking journey.

ROSE MARIE MEUWISSEN

BIO

Rose Marie Meuwissen, a first-generation Norwegian American born and raised in Minnesota, always tries to incorporate her Norwegian heritage into her writing. After receiving a BA in Marketing from

Concordia University, a Masters in Creative Writing from Hamline University soon followed. Minnesota is still where she calls home.

She has traveled around the world, including Scandinavia, but still has many places to see, enjoys attending Scandinavian events, writing conferences and is usually busy writing Contemporary or Viking Time Travel Romances and Norwegian Traditions Children's Books.

Visit her at:

www.rosemariemeuwissen.com

www.realnorwegianseatlutefisk.com.

NOVELS:

Taking Chances—a contemporary romance novel set in Minnesota and Arizona.

Married by Saturday—a contemporary romance novel set in Minnesota and Montana.

Looking for Mr. Right—a contemporary internet dating romance novel set on Prior Lake in Minnesota—***Coming soon!***

NOVELLAS:

Annika—A Christmas Romance—a contemporary romance set in Minnesota with a Nordic theme during the Christmas Holidays.

Skol! Viking Blonde Ale—a contemporary romance set in Minnesota at an Autumn festival complete with a fortune teller, ale and Vikings!

Choosing to Live—a Norwegian woman's journey during WWII to survive the Nazi Occupation of Norway—***Coming soon!***

ANTHOLOGIES:

A Date for Valentine's Day—a short romance set at Lafayette Country Club on Lake Minnetonka, Minnesota available in the anthology, *Romancing the Lakes of Minnesota—Valentine's Day.*

Dance of Love—a short romance set at the Renaissance Fair in Shakopee, Minnesota, available in the anthology, *Festivals of Love.*

Dancing in the Moonlight—a short romance set on Mille Lacs Lake, Minnesota available in the anthology, *Love in the Land of Lakes.*

A Kiss Under the Northern Lights—a short romance set in Ely, Minnesota available in the anthology, *Northern Kisses.*

CHILDREN'S BOOKS—REAL NORWEGIAN'S SERIES:

Real Norwegians Eat Lutefisk—a Children's book about the tradition of Lutefisk presented in both English and Norwegian.

Real Norwegians Eat Rømmegrøt—the second Children's book in the series about the tradition of Rømmegrøt presented in both English and Norwegian.

Real Norwegians Eat Lefse—the third Children's book in the series about the tradition of Lefse presented in both English and Norwegian.

Real Norwegians Eat Krumkake—the fourth Children's book in the series about the tradition of Krumkake presented in both English and Norwegian—*Coming next!*

NOVELETTES—COMING SOON!

Hot Summer Nights—a Summer romance set in Prior Lake, Minnesota on Prior Lake.

Railroad Ties—an Autumn romance set in Two Harbors, Minnesota on Lake Superior.

Blizzard of Love—a Winter romance set in Lutsen, Minnesota on Lake Superior.

Nor-Way to Love—a Spring romance set in Minneapolis, Minnesota on Lake Harriet.

Old Yule Log Fires—a Christmas romance set in Excelsior, Minnesota on Lake Minnetonka.

MICRO-MINI NOVELETTE—COMING SOON!

Christmas Notes—a collection of Christmas prose poems to warm the heart during the Christmas season.

www.ingramcontent.com/pod-product-compliance
Lightning Source LLC
Chambersburg PA
CBHW050800250626
47155CB00005B/2147